D0402964

THE LEOPARD IS LOOSE

THE LEOPARD IS LOOSE

Stephen Harrigan

ALFRED A. KNOPF

NEW YORK 2022

THIS IS A BORZOI BOOK
PUBLISHED BY ALFRED A. KNOPF

Published in the United States by Alfred A. Knopf,
a division of Penguin Random House LLC, New York,
and distributed in Canada by Penguin Random House
Canada Limited, Toronto.

www.aaknopf.com

Knopf, Borzoi Books, and the colophon are registered
trademarks of Penguin Random House LLC.

Library of Congress Cataloging-in-Publication Data
Names: Harrigan, Stephen, [date] author.
Title: The leopard is loose : a novel / Stephen Harrigan.
Description: First Edition. | New York : Alfred A. Knopf, 2022.
Identifiers: LCCN 2021028338 (print) | LCCN 2021028339 (ebook) |
ISBN 9780525655770 (hardcover) | ISBN 9780525655787 (ebook)
Classification: LCC PS3558.A626 L46 2022 (print) |
LCC PS3558.A626 (ebook) | DDC 813/.54—dc23
LC record available at https://lccn.loc.gov/2021028338
LC ebook record available at https://lccn.loc.gov/2021028339

This is a work of fiction. Names, characters, places, and incidents
either are the product of the author's imagination or are used
fictitiously. Any resemblance to actual persons, living or dead,
events, or locales is entirely coincidental.

Jacket images: (boy) RooM the Agency/Alamy;
(fence) TheArtist/Getty; (leopard) Robert Adrian Hillman/Alamy;
(paper) Pampalini/Getty Images
Jacket design by Jenny Carrow

Manufactured in the United States of America
First Edition

A Note to Readers

There really was a sensational leopard escape from the Lincoln Park Zoo in Oklahoma City in 1950. To take advantage of some of my own childhood memories, I have moved the event forward in time several years, and have done some minor tinkering with the chronology of certain TV shows or All-Star baseball games. I have also set this novel to some degree within the matrix of my own extended family at a time when I, like Grady McClarty, was five years old. But *The Leopard Is Loose* is very much a fictional enterprise, and especially so when it comes to the depiction of the two uncles in this novel. The relentless demands of dramatic structure have required me to invent characters and saddle them with various flaws and afflictions, but I am anxious that these fictional presences never be confused with the uncles—four of them, in real life—who were such steadfast and selfless figures in the lives of two fatherless boys. To them—Joe Berney, Bob Berney, Paul ("D.D.") Berney, and Mike Berney—this book is lovingly dedicated.

THE LEOPARD IS LOOSE

I

To the Oklahoma Historical Society:

My name is Grady McClarty. I am seventy years old, the retired general manager of Wolfcamp Chevrolet in Midland, Texas, where I have resided for most of my life. I am writing in response to a request I received from one of your archivists, Marguerite Talkingthunder, to record an oral history of the "great leopard escape" that occurred in Oklahoma City when I was living there as a young boy in the early 1950s.

I hope it won't disappoint you if I provide a written reminiscence instead of an oral one. I ordered a little digital recorder from Amazon and did my best to tell this story into it. But I've always found it difficult to order my thoughts when speaking out loud, and even though I tried recording myself in the garage, out of the hearing of my wife, Jeannette, I still felt too conspicuous and self-conscious. For one thing, this is an intimate story about a little boy and his family, and trying to tell it out loud meant always having to resist the temptation to make it bigger, to inflate it with a meaning it didn't have then, and I assume does not have now. (Although of course the leopard escape was at the time a very big deal, and I and my family played a part in it, which is the reason you asked for my memories in the first place.)

This might turn out to be a lengthy document. Your request had the effect of knocking the lid off a big box of memories, and reminding me that despite or because of a lifetime in the car business, I've always imagined a parallel existence for myself as a writer. A strain of artistic aspiration, mostly frustrated by real-life demands, runs through my mother's side of the family, going back at least to my great-grandmother, who wrote a privately published, surprisingly colorful history of the Kansas county where her Czech ancestors settled. That particular family trait didn't spare me. I was an English major at the University of Texas until some sort of reality panic—a sense that I was whimsically indulging myself in a hobby and not investing in a real career—caused me to switch to business. But I never gave up reading. I'm the ringleader of a Midland book club that has met every month for forty years. My children, after I die, will one day open a locked drawer in the desk of my home office and find a puzzling artifact: a dozen old-time floppy disks that contain an unfinished and hopelessly unfocused historical novel about the early days of oil exploration in the Permian Basin.

And now it seems you've given me something else, something closer to home, to write about. I've reached an age where looking into my past, trying to sort out who everybody was back then, and what they were thinking, and how I came to be who I am, feels not just natural but sort of urgent. I don't know why this should be so, particularly in the case of someone like me who has lived an utterly ordinary life and has nothing exciting to report. But there does seem to be a kind of summing-up instinct that hits people around this stage of life, if we're lucky enough to have made it this far—a sudden interest in family origins and ancestors and, especially, the unsolved mysteries of childhood that we didn't even know at the time were mysteries.

I was only five years old when the leopard escaped, so you'll have to take that into account when judging the accuracy of these recollections. I searched the Internet under "childhood memories" recently and it seems to be the case that people can remember highly significant or highly emotional events from their childhoods—losing a parent, getting a dog, moving to a new house—as early as three years of age, but that most real memories don't form until about four and a half. I suppose that puts me in the zone of reliability, at least somewhat. But memories are mostly about the events that for one reason or another seized our attention; they're not a continuous record of everything that happened in between. What I retain from those distant years is a more or less random accumulation of textures, smells, gestures, tones of voice, feelings of safety or fear, a strong sense of a particular place experienced with a child's hazy awareness of time. In order to write all this down in a way that makes sense, I'm going to have to pretend that I was observing things more clearly and listening more carefully than I really was. You should, for instance, treat the conversations that I recount here in quotation marks as only an earnest effort to approximate what might actually have been said. It's up to you to decide whether any of this can be thought of as history, and not merely fiction, but I wanted you to know it's as conscientious an effort as I could make with the fragments of memory available to me. I was just a young boy; I wasn't taking notes.

This all happened in the summer of 1952. My mother and my brother, Danny, and I lived in a two-bedroom backyard apartment on NW 34th Street that backed up to a sprawling public park. In front of us, across a small patch of fenced-in yard, was the two-story prairie-style house where my grandparents and my aunt Vivian lived, and above us lived my two uncles, in a garage apartment whose main room was dominated by a pool table.

It added up to a kind of family compound. My grandparents' house, where they had largely raised their children, was erected before World War I. The addition in back—our place and the bachelor apartment above it—was several decades newer. My grandfather had it built a few years after the end of the next war so that my suddenly widowed mother and her infant son and another son on the way (me) would have a place to live when they came home to Oklahoma City.

I suppose it was a common enough arrangement at the time, when so many young married men had been killed in the war, and so many young mothers were left without husbands and had to be absorbed back into the homes they thought they had left behind to make families of their own. It was certainly no novelty to me or to Danny. Like any children, we accepted the world we were born into without a thought. In our case, it was a world whose center was a mother who was—I realize now—still unsteady from grief and shock. We called her

Bethie, because there were so many people in our household who called her that—our grandparents and aunt and uncles—that the words "Mother" or "Mom" never had much of a chance to enter our vocabulary.

I've gone back through all the newspaper accounts about the leopard escape. There's a clear beginning and end to that story, and I'll try to write this so that it tracks along with the larger narrative and has a beginning and an end as well. The experienced writer I once hoped to become would have a better idea of a compelling place to start, but I'm just going to have to follow my instincts and hope that my memories—my own story—will end up being relevant and useful to the Historical Society.

So I'll begin on a summer night that was probably a week or so before Oklahoma City went insane, when the little world I inhabited still seemed orderly and peaceful. It was dark, and it must have been late, otherwise when I woke up in the bedroom I shared with Danny I would have still heard the *thock-thock-thock* of tennis balls echoing in the summer night from the park behind our house. I was awake because I had to tee-tee, as we said back in the 1950s. The bathroom was midway in the hallway between our bedroom and our mother's, but when I got out of bed and took a step into the hallway I saw that the light was off and the open door leading to the bathroom was like the entrance to a chasm. Our room had a nightlight, a translucent plastic six-shooter set into a holster with the word "Hoppy" on it, and a depiction of the face of the white-haired cowboy hero Hopalong Cassidy beneath his enormous black hat. But the night-light's glow was as weak as the lens of a flashlight with dying batteries, and it didn't reach much beyond the door to our bedroom.

The hallway wasn't completely dark, though. There was some moonlight seeping in from the bathroom window, just enough illumination to highlight contours and create shadows. And there was something terrifying lying on the floor in the middle of the hallway—a black, shapeless, menacing entity. There must have been a few swaying tree branches outside the bathroom window that, with the moonlight filtering through them, created the effect that the thing was moving. Moving very slightly and quietly, like it was breathing. Breathing and waiting, ready to snatch me if I entered the hallway or tried to run past it to the safety of my mother's room.

I was paralyzed. Danny was asleep in the room behind me. He was a year older and I was still young enough to think of him as my protector. But if I called out to him the thing would hear my voice, and if I turned around and tried to wake him up the thing would sense my movement. As it was, it hadn't yet noticed I was there. But if I moved or made a sound, it would get me.

I must have stood there for a long time, quietly shaking with fear, until I began to try to convince myself that if I ran fast enough, and kept low enough, I could get past that shapeless monster. I could sprint down the hallway to the room where Bethie slept, slam the door behind me, and leap into her bed, where I would be safe beneath her green satin bedspread. She had let me sleep there before, after I had had my tonsils taken out and was suffering from a bad sore throat. If she knew how scared I was she would let me stay there again.

I would be okay if I could only reach the open door at the end of the hallway. I got ready, told myself "Run!"; but before I could work up the nerve to do so I realized the thing had already spotted me. It was looking at me. It didn't have eyes, but it somehow saw me. It knew I was going to try to run past it. I was convinced that it knew everything I was thinking. I wouldn't be able to make it even halfway down the hallway before it grabbed me, and now I was sure that if I turned around and went back to bed it would slither in pursuit, creep over me, and smother me.

I continued to stand there motionless, or as motionless as I could make myself, for several more excruciating minutes, with my full bladder only sharpening my sense of urgency and terror. I might have stayed there, frozen, all night, if the spell hadn't been broken by the sound of a car pulling into the driveway. The beams of its headlights swept across the curtained picture window of our little living room and reached into the hallway.

I heard car doors slamming and then the voices of my uncles, Frank and Emmett. Emmett was saying, "For Christ's sake, don't let the folks see you like this"; and though I don't remember hearing Frank say anything in reply I could sense his drunken annoyance at being lectured to by his younger, less drunk, and more fretful brother.

Emmett was pleading with him not to wake up Bethie and the boys, but Frank had already opened the front door that led upstairs to our uncles' garage apartment. He pounded on our door, which opened onto the same interior stairway. "Bethie!" he shouted. "Danny! Grady! Time to wake up! Time to see the goddamn comet!"

Frank's ranting and pounding woke my mother up, and all at once the light in the hallway came on and I saw her at the door of her bedroom. She was blinking and tying the belt of her bathrobe, and there was a bouncing curl of brown hair over one of her eyes. "What are you doing up, honey?" she said in an anxious and confused voice when she saw me standing at the other end of the hallway.

She walked toward me and, on the way, casually bent down to pick up a dark brown raincoat that had fallen from the coat rack and was lying on the floor. This was the pulsing creature that had been threatening me in the darkness. Danny was awake by then as well, and Bethie told him to stay with me while I finally went to the bathroom.

"I'm just going outside to talk to the boys for a minute," she said. Still in her robe, she hurried out the front door into the summer night to confront her brothers.

"Hurry up and teetee!" Danny told me as I stood over the rim of the toilet. "I want to see what's happening." Impatient and curious, he reached out for the handle and flushed before I had even finished, and then the two of us raced across the narrow living room, climbed onto the couch in front of the picture window, and parted the curtains.

At first there were just the three of them—Bethie and Frank and Emmett. They stood arguing in front of Frank's black Fleetline, the 1949 fastback model with an external sunshade over the front window that looked like the bill of a scrunched-down ball cap. (Sorry—even though I'm retired I haven't purged my mind of all its Chevrolet lore.) My mother would have been thirty-two in 1952, Frank a year older, Emmett not yet out of his twenties. In other words, young—at least the way I look back on them now. But at the time their angry voices and their defensive postures made them seem to us as if they were oppressed by inscrutable adult burdens that had been bearing down upon them since the beginning of time.

Frank was still going on in a loud voice about the comet, arguing with my mother about it, incensed that she would prefer to have us in bed and asleep when the newspaper said there was going to be a spectacular occurrence in the sky any minute, something that Danny and I would never forget. But we were less likely to ever forget the sight of our uncle Frank stumbling about in the driveway, swinging his arms and lecturing our mother in a voice that was loud enough to wake the neighbors. I mentioned earlier that he was drunk, but at that moment I had no idea what being drunk meant, nor had I yet seen anyone in that condition. So Frank was a stranger to us that night, an unnerving one. In our life up until that time, he was always a quiet adult presence, so still and composed that his slightest movement drew your attention: the confident way he would shift the cigarette from his right to his left hand before rising from a chair to shake hands with somebody, or the way he made the habitual gesture of men in that baggy-pants era, hitching up his trousers at the knees just before sitting down again. He was taller than Emmett and stood straighter. He kept his brown hair short and tightly combed. He had been an infantry sergeant in the war, and though I didn't know that fact about him at the time it made sense to me when I learned it later. He had a natural presumption of command.

Which was why it was so frightening to see all that composure disappear without warning, to hear the unfamiliar sarcasm in his voice, the almost bullying tone in which he was now lecturing our mother on how to raise her children. Bethie was facing away from us and I couldn't see the tears that must have been in her eyes, but her feet were planted and her back was rigid—she wasn't going to stand for this behavior. Frank may have been her older brother but she had outranked him in the war. He may have been a sergeant but she, an Army nurse, had been a lieutenant. My mother liked to tell about how, when they were briefly stationed at the same base in California, he had had to salute her as she walked by him on the way to the hospital.

"Come on, Frank," Emmett said as he pulled on his brother's arm, "just calm down a little bit. Let's go upstairs like Bethie says."

Frank swatted away Emmett's arm as vigorously as if he meant to take a swing at him, then stalked off to the center of the driveway and looked up at the sky with his head craned back. In the moonlight I could see his pale neck and his Adam's apple slowly moving up and down.

He stood that way for a long time, while Emmett glanced apologetically at my mother and she stood there angrily in her bathrobe with her arms crossed. "There it is! There it is!" Frank finally called out. He pleaded one more time for Bethie to get Danny and me, and then he sprinted to the other end of the driveway to the main house, calling out that he was going to wake up his parents and our aunt Vivian. "You two might as well come outside," Bethie said to us in a defeated voice when she finally came back and opened the door to our apartment. "But after you see the comet you're going right back to bed, and I mean it."

So in a few moments there we all were. Our grandfather had just emerged from the back door, his normally slicked-back hair bristling out at the sides, glaring in judgment at his older son through the owlish lenses of his glasses. Behind him was our grandmother, with her familiar look of confusion and impending tragedy, and Vivian, young and untethered and unbothered, always delighted by the prospect of something unexpected or semiforbidden.

Then for a while all the noise and rancor and childhood terror of that night were put aside, as we all stared upward, barely able to see the faint white smudge of the comet slowly making its way across the Oklahoma sky. I remember Frank lifting me in his arms and pointing the comet out to me, patiently waiting until I was finally able to track it. He was suddenly calm now, my protective uncle again, no longer the frightening stranger who had arrived with such turmoil in the middle of the night while my feverish imagination was conjuring up a raincoat monster in the hallway.

2

We were a Catholic family, in the way families were Catholic way back in the middle of the twentieth century. There were crucifixes in every room of my grandparents' house, along with a little plaster holy-water font just below the old-fashioned push-button light switch in their bedroom. And hanging on the wall opposite their bed, where they could see it every morning when they woke up, was a framed illustration of Jesus, one hand raised in benediction, the other pointing to the Sacred Heart throbbing outside of his chest. On the top shelf of the closet was the feathery bicorn hat of my grandfather's Knights of Columbus uniform, along with his sash and ceremonial sword.

It probably goes without saying that in a household like that, Mass on Sunday was mandatory. It must have been on a Saturday night that my uncles came home drunk and Frank had bullied the whole family into a late-night search for a comet, because I remember seeing him and Emmett in the main house that next morning when we came in for breakfast. (As children too young to receive communion, we were the only members of the household who did not have to fast before going to church.) My uncles were dressed for Mass and wilting under the silent rebuke of their father as he pretended to read *The Daily Oklahoman*. They both looked miserable, hungover and ashamed, and the fact that the Sunday morning prohibitions denied them even the solace of coffee must have made them feel even worse.

Danny and I were feeling pretty bad ourselves. It was a Sunday morning in an era when people dressed up to go downtown, to fly on airplanes, and above all to go to church. That meant that we were wearing our short-pant suits of intolerably itchy wool and facing an ordeal of droning Latin and suffocating incense.

"You two can just stop pouting right now," Bethie said as we pleaded with her to stay home. "We're all going to Mass and that's it."

Her temper was short this morning, no doubt the result of the sleep she had lost the night before. Danny and I were probably more disoriented than we realized by Frank's behavior, and I was still caught in the undertow of that waking dream about the hallway monster. That must have been why she had allowed us to sleep the rest of the night in her bed.

"You boys look pretty sharp this morning," Emmett said to Danny and me with a gloomy smile. He was shorter and slighter than Frank. His abundant black hair made him look younger than he was, and the way my mother looked at him—fond and disappointed—made him look younger still. She had been only five or six when he was born, but she had probably already been stamped with the maternal personality and the rigorous sense of duty that had disposed her to think of her younger brother as a child who would always need her protection.

The last person to appear that morning was my aunt Vivian, floating down from her bedroom upstairs, smelling of some fashionable bygone perfume whose fragrance still hovers, just out of reach, in my olfactory memory. She was young and slim and at that point in her career a secretary to the vice president of an oil-and-gas company. Some of the tennis balls I habitually heard at night from the park while I was in bed were lobbed from her racket or that of one of her tennis partners— either another young secretary or one of the indistinct men who would turn up at the house to take her out for a date.

On a typical Sunday we all endured Mass and then piled into one or more cars and went on a drive. The usual routine was to head south toward downtown through our relatively modest neighborhood to check out the houses in Heritage Hills, venerable brick mansions that looked to me as ancient as medieval castles, though the oldest of them at that time was less than fifty years old, built a decade or so after the Land Run that had created Oklahoma City in one frantic day in 1889. We would cruise down Classen Boulevard, my brother and I standing un-seat-belted between our grandparents in the front seat, past Kamp's grocery store and Herman's seafood restaurant and the tiny, triangular brick package store with the towering concrete milk bottle on its roof, and then make our way slowly downtown—the grand old downtown that used to be there, before most of it was torn down in the 1960s in a misguided urban-renewal project. My grandfather would slow down as we passed the Katz drugstore so that Danny and I could take in the big sign out front depicting a black cat whose wide whiskers sprouted diagonally outward from his face in a way that mirrored the bow tie at his neck. He would slow down again as he passed the showroom of his Chevrolet dealership farther down on Main Street, the new models of Stylelines and Fleetlines behind the picture windows looking to me as if they were purposefully resting, like the living but immobile animals we saw in the reptile house at the zoo.

Speaking of the zoo, that place is very much at the center of this story, and as I remember things it was also close to the center of my childhood life. Our uncles took us there often enough that it was a Sunday ritual every bit as familiar as, and far more welcome than, church at Our Lady of Perpetual Help. We certainly went there the day I'm talking about, that afternoon after our Sunday drive. It was always Frank and Emmett who took us. On Sundays my mother worked a weekend shift at St. Anthony's Hospital, Vivian would be out to the movies or water skiing at Lake Overholser, and my grandmother at home cooking Sunday dinner while my grandfather watched a baseball game on his day off on the fuzzy Magnavox television in the living room.

The trip to the zoo that Sunday was outwardly the same as always, though as Danny and I sat in the car at the front curb, waiting to go, our uncles were still at the front door, listening with their heads slightly down, hands in their pockets, as our grandfather delivered a lecture. We were too far away to hear his words. I could see his face, though, and hear the occasional sharp syllable of rebuke, and I was scared. Not of my grandfather, not of my uncles, but of something confusing and destabilizing in our world that had until that point been kept away from us.

My grandfather finally withdrew into the house and shut the door, and our uncles turned and hurried down the front porch steps and into the car, Frank behind the steering wheel and Emmett in the passenger seat.

"Well, if he plans to talk to us like that again," Frank said, "he'd better be ready to—"

"Cut it out," Emmett cautioned him. "Little pitchers have big ears."

Frank gave the steering wheel a hard rap with the heel of his hand and then left it at that. He turned to us, smiling.

"Either of you little pitchers want to drive?"

He let Danny and me take turns, as usual, sitting in his lap with our hands on the steering wheel as we headed east on 36th Street. It was only five or six miles from our house to the zoo, but it always seemed to me that we were traveling much farther, past the realm of our own neighborhood and into strange territory where the trees were thicker and the houses sparser, and where undeveloped tracts of red dirt seemed to announce the edge of the world.

We knew our way around the zoo, starting with the monkey island just inside the entrance, where inside a big circular pit rhesus monkeys clambered through the portholes and up the rigging of an upended pirate ship that had been built to look as if it were sliding stern-first into the ocean. We usually watched the monkeys for a while and then headed off to see the zoo's only elephant, a lonely young female named Judy. She was five years old, my age, and so I imagined that some sort of friendship or special connection existed between us, and that she recognized me among the crowd of kids always gathered in front of her as she slipped her trunk through the diamond-shaped openings of a chain-link fence. Emmett bought us bags of unshelled peanuts, and when her trunk swung in our direction we placed a peanut in each of her nostrils and watched as she rhythmically swept them into her mouth.

After checking in on Judy, we sped through the frightening part of the zoo, along a sidewalk that led past a giant aviary where owls stared down at us with unnerving scrutiny, and where wild, uncaged geese almost as tall as me mobbed us as we passed. They were so aggressive that I had to cling to Frank's pant leg as he shooed them off—until we were finally able to reach the safety of the wooden dock that jutted out past the shoreline of the little lake at the edge of the zoo.

I liked to stand at the end of the dock watching the kiddie train as it traveled in and out of the trees on the other side of the lake. When I looked down at the water, I had a dizzying sensation that I was speeding over the lake's surface. Since the dock and I remained in the same place, this confounded me and made me search for an answer to why I was standing still and racing forward at the same time. I was too innocent to grasp that the sensation of movement was generated by the sight of the wind-driven ripples on the surface of the lake as they passed beneath the dock. It was one of those simple, obvious things that are not obvious at all to the mind of a five-year-old child. At that age I was assembling my own answers, my own logic, to try to explain an incomprehensible world. It was why I believed that Hopalong Cassidy and the Cisco Kid existed as real black-and-white beings somewhere in the box behind the TV screen and were actively putting on a show in real time. Or why I believed that when my aunt Vivian put on a record by Rosemary Clooney or Nat King Cole, it brought to life not just a voice but a real singer trapped inside a world of flattened vinyl.

I was still staring into the water, mystified by the speedboat velocity I was experiencing, when Frank said, "You boys sit down for a minute. Emmett and I need to talk to you."

We obediently sat down on the dock, looking up at our two uncles in their short-sleeved sport shirts with their Lucky Strike and Old Gold packs visible through the thin fabric of their chest pockets. Their wide-legged pants flared a bit in the same breeze that was sending the wavelets under the dock. We thought that Frank was going to speak, but he looked uncertain and uncomfortable, and with a subtle head toss he handed off the task to his younger brother.

Emmett hesitated for a moment, but he was better at speaking to us than Frank was, and I suppose they both knew it.

"We just wanted to make sure," he said, "that you boys are okay."

When we didn't say anything, he went on. "Frank and I may have given you a scare last night."

We didn't know what to say to that, either.

"So," Emmett asked, crouching down to our level and speaking in a soft voice. "Did we scare you?"

"No," Danny said. Emmett turned to me and I said no as well, though I had indeed been scared.

"That's good. See, we'd been drinking maybe a little too much, and when you do that you can act kind of crazy sometimes—can't you, Frank?"

"Sometimes," Frank agreed.

"But there's nothing wrong with us now," Emmett said. "It's just a normal day at the zoo. And the last thing we want to do is upset you boys or upset your mother. She's been through enough already. Losing your father was a pretty big blow to her, you know."

We knew, but we didn't. Nobody ever talked about our father. We knew his name was Burt. He had been a pilot in the war, a fighter pilot. The words "fighter pilot" intrigued us and made him sound exotic, but the fact that he was our father was an abstraction when there were so many living men around us, like our grandfather, or like Frank and Emmett. Burt might as well have existed a hundred years ago.

"It was even worse for her, probably," Frank said. Unlike Emmett, he wasn't crouched down in front of us, meeting our eyes. He was still standing, with one hand in his pocket jingling his keys as he looked off over the lake. "Because he made it all the way through the war—even got shot down— with hardly a scratch. Then when it looked like everything was going to be fine . . ."

He didn't finish the thought, just gave what I would now recognize as a fatalistic shrug. Our father had been a test pilot after the war, and had died when the plane he was flying broke apart in mid-flight. That was a few months before I was born and when Danny was less than a year old. I didn't know what the "war" was—it was just a word that seemed to have more meaning than other words—and I didn't know how the time that came after it was different. I was aware, I think, that the world had not been born along with me, that something had been here before my existence, and that something long and terrible had taken place. In my mind there was a kind of image of the time before my birth. I saw it as a strange dark smudge hovering in a gray eternity.

"Anyway," Emmett said, after a confused pause, "we just wanted to say that everything's fine. Nothing for you boys to worry about. Okay?"

We nodded our heads, because that was what our uncles seemed to want, and then we were off again on our usual circuit of the zoo, through the reptile house and the primate building and along the lakeside walkway that passed a row of enclosures built by the Works Progress Administration in the 1930s, and that nearly twenty years later still represented a forward-looking style of how to exhibit captive animals. Instead of cages there were big, open pits that backed up against jumbled boulders made of concrete. To prevent escape there was a moat at the front of the pit, and in front of the moat a sheer wall that led up to a wooden rail fence where zoo visitors stood and looked down.

There was a polar bear in one of those pits, a thin-looking polar bear. His white fur was always tinted an unhealthy-looking green, maybe from the algae or the chlorine that was in the water in the moat. His behavior was always the same. It was neurotically precise. He made a few swaying steps to his left, turned and did the same in the other direction, slipped headfirst into the moat, slipped out, shook the water off his body, then went through the same unvarying paces again and again. He did that no doubt for all his life, an animal tortured by confinement and isolation, though at the time I don't think it occurred to many people that this metronomic movement was particularly unusual. It was, to us, just the silly way that a polar bear behaved.

There was another bear in the next enclosure, a sun bear, whose fur was all black except for a golden U-shaped patch on his chest. He sat all day on his haunches, slowly waving his arms, waiting for children to throw him the peanuts left over from feeding Judy, the elephant. If a peanut landed close enough, he would make the effort to bend over and scoop it up with his paw, but if it was farther than a few paces away he would just write it off and continue sitting upright, counting on the next one to land closer.

Farther down along the row was the leopard pit. Normally I would have walked by it with only a glance, since leopards were not as imposing as bears and were often hard to spot in those giant open enclosures. I wouldn't remember even seeing them that day if it hadn't been for the extraordinary thing that happened. As we were walking past the pit a sense of agitation coming from below made me pause at the rail fence and look down. One of the two leopards was motionless and almost out of sight, asleep in a shady declivity at the base of the enclosure. But the other one was on his feet and pacing—pacing not with the resigned, synchronized dance steps of the polar bear, but with an urgent purpose. I wouldn't learn until later that this leopard had been captured in India only a few weeks before. At the time we encountered him, he had been living in this pit in the Oklahoma City Zoo for just three or four days. He was still actively bewildered, still searching for a way out, unlike the other leopard—a female—who had long ago resigned herself to the futility of escape.

Danny and I climbed up onto the first log rail of the fence so that we could get a better look. We weren't there long. From such a distance, the creature in the pit wasn't all that interesting to watch. We were about to climb down from the fence and move on when the leopard sprang at us, launching himself off the ground in an eerily fluid motion that we had not seen him preparing for. One moment he was on the ground, the next he was aloft, soaring weightlessly toward me with his front legs outstretched and claws revealed as if he were intending to grab me. In almost the same instant I was airborne as well, snatched off the fence and jerked backward by Frank. Emmett did the same with Danny, and I heard him shout, "Whoa there!"

The two uncles were laughing, joking about what a close call it had been, though they assumed it had not been close at all—the pit was so deep there was no apparent way the leopard could have jumped all the way out of it.

Danny and I laughed too, excited as much by the almost violent way our uncles had snatched us off the fence as we were by the animal soaring fluidly toward us.

"I think that leopard wants out of there," Frank said.

It was strange that I wasn't scared, not then. But the image of that animal with his arms outstretched in midair, with his eyes on me, settled deep into my mind and my memory, waiting to be released the next time I had a nightmare.

3

I mentioned there was a park behind our house. The park wasn't that large, about fifteen acres stretching between Classen Boulevard at one end—where there was a multitiered fountain, a memorial to the dead of World War I—and Western Avenue at the other, where there stood a redbrick monument to an inscrutable somebody named Shakespeare. Only fifteen acres, but the park seemed to us children like a whole world that could never be fully explored.

At the end of our driveway, next to the garage to which our apartment was attached, a hedge ran along the border between our property and the park. There was a gap in the hedge, and in the gap was a gate with two miniature crouching dogs on top, like sphinxes guarding some great secret space. To me, the gate was a magic portal. Beyond it a grassy slope opened into the vast center of the park. The park was big enough to contain, in addition to the fountain and the Shakespeare monument, a swimming pool, the courts where Vivian played tennis, and a meandering gully that once had been a creek.

There was also a bandstand, or at least a slab of concrete that had been poured on top of a rocky outcropping on the far bank of the dried-up creek. The visit to the zoo I just described must have taken place close to the Fourth of July, because I remember that a few days later our whole family walked down to the park to sit on blankets and listen to a brass band playing patriotic music.

I was wearing a striped T-shirt and a pair of brown corduroy shorts with the figure of a cowboy twirling a lasso embroidered on the two rear pockets. That's just a random memory fragment that has nothing to do with anything, but at my age such tangible recollections are as precious as family photographs. They're like the mile markers along a stretch of Oklahoma highway with no scenery—something to grab hold of so that the whole trip doesn't just vanish from your memory even as it's taking place.

We were all there sitting on blankets—my grandparents, my mother, Danny and I, Vivian, and our uncles. I remember the feeling of leaning against Bethie as she ran her fingers lightly up and down my spine—a feeling of security that came partly from my mother's touch and partly from the realization that she was relaxed, that the grief and anxiety and responsibility that I could somehow sense was always present in her had evaporated, at least for the moment. Frank and Emmett were relaxed, too, drinking beer, smoking, listening impassively to the stirring music. It was far past our strict bedtime, but the summer daylight still lingered, and nobody seemed to care that evening whether we went to sleep or not.

"Don't look now," Vivian said to her sister during a lull in the music, "but I think somebody's heading our way."

I saw my mother turn her head and could sense her mood brightening even more. A man was walking toward us. He was only about forty-five, but I didn't know that at the time. To Danny and me, his graying hair would have made him seem ancient if it weren't for something lively and knowing about him. He was slender and, in a time when men tended to turn out in slacks and sport shirts for even informal occasions like this one, he seemed well-dressed. But there was nothing fussy or mannered about his appearance. It was just part of an over-all air of confidence.

Vivian sprang immediately to her feet as he approached and said, "Well, hello there, Hugh!" So that was his name. I saw my grandfather, then only in his early fifties, close to Hugh's age, rise as well, and watched as the two men shook hands and introduced themselves. Hugh then shook hands with Frank and Emmett. I could tell they were sizing him up, that they regarded his appearance in the midst of this family outing as something of a big deal.

I didn't learn until much later in my life that Hugh was the friend of a man Vivian was dating at the time, and that this seemingly casual encounter in the park was in fact something she had painstakingly orchestrated so that Hugh—unmarried, a devout if worldly Catholic—could meet my widowed mother.

But I could sense at once that there was something momentous going on, something that had the potential to change the world I had been born into and was very much accustomed to. It was why I was instantly suspicious of Hugh, and resentful of the way that my mother looked at him and that he looked at her when Vivian introduced them, and of the way he shook hands with Danny and me and told us what good-looking boys we were and how happy he was to meet us, and what a fine family we belonged to.

"Well, I'll let you all get back to the concert," he said. He was careful to preserve the illusion that this was just a casual, happenstance meeting in the park. He had the tact not to draw it out, though I remember being very sure that we had not seen the last of him. I was also aware of the silent moment that passed between my mother and her sister—a kind of "Didn't I tell you?" expression on Vivian's face and the flustered but noncommittal look that was my mother's reply.

A few minutes later, as the band continued to play, an airplane flew over the park. It came in low, very low, its engine roaring. Next to me, Emmett cringed and jerked his head upward. For just a moment, it was as if my uncle's familiar face had disappeared and been replaced by a generic human expression of blank panic. But it was only for a moment. My grandfather saw what was happening, gripped Emmett's shoulder with his hand, and whispered, "It's all right, son." And then Emmett was back to himself, watching with the rest of us as the plane released hundreds of balloons over the park.

I was spellbound at the sight of those multicolored balloons. The rich, fading sunlight made them glow like light bulbs, and the music coming from the bandstand seemed to have been written to orchestrate their slow fall to earth.

Danny and I joined the rest of the kids in the park in a frenzied chase after the balloons, tracking them as they fell, trying to predict where they would touch ground. Most of the kids were older and faster, and every balloon I tried to retrieve was snatched away before I could reach it. But Danny got one, and when I returned to our blanket, crestfallen, I saw Frank standing there, holding a balloon that he had snared from the sky before it landed. He handed it to me and told me to hold on to its string while he popped it with the end of his cigarette. Inside was a slip of paper that was an advertisement for a local shoe store, with a coupon for a free ice-cream cone. The airplane that had released these balloons was still flying above us, still very much in evidence, but that didn't detract from the sensation I felt that the balloons and the ice-cream coupons were not a mercenary ploy but the gift of some invisible sky-dwelling being.

Much later that night, long after we had gone to bed, I felt Danny shaking me—almost punching me—as he whispered. "Wake up!" I opened my eyes in confusion, in the middle of our familiar room, with the weakly glowing Hopalong Cassidy night-light illuminating the green chest of drawers at the foot of our beds.

"Listen!" he said.

I listened, conditioned to follow any command from my big brother. From above, from our uncles' garage apartment, we heard the strangest sound: an anguished, piercing, wordless cry, almost a whoop, repeating over and over. We heard our uncle Frank's voice saying "C'mon now! C'mon!" but the sound didn't stop. Then we heard our mother's bedroom door suddenly open, and her footsteps as she hurried through the hallway and through our living room, then out the door that opened to the stairway leading to Frank and Emmett's apartment. She was moving so fast that she didn't even close the door behind her, and her bare feet sounded like they were bounding up the stairs two or three steps at a time.

"I'm going up there," Danny said.

I had no real choice but to go with him. I didn't want to be alone in our apartment with so much turmoil going on upstairs that I couldn't understand. So I followed behind Danny as he climbed the stairs. We moved slowly, nervously, one step at a time. The steps were covered with old-fashioned rubber stair runners that—to my acute childhood senses—gave off a rich vulcanized smell. Danny stopped at the open door at the top of the stairs and we peered cautiously inside. The apartment was basically one big room with a bathroom and a small galley kitchen at one end. Most of the space was taken up by a pool table and Emmett's drafting table, but the room was big enough to accommodate two narrow beds—almost cots—at the far end, where Frank and Emmett slept.

At first we didn't see anything, but when we dared to peer in a little closer we saw our mother sitting on one of the beds holding Emmett in her arms and making the same shushing sounds that she made to calm us when we were upset. He wasn't crying, but he was shaking, and his chest was heaving, and even in the faint light cast by a nearby table lamp we could see that sweat was pouring down his forehead almost in a steady flow.

"You're here," Bethie was saying to him. "You're right here with us."

Emmett nodded his head, agreeing, understanding, but still caught in the grip of something that wasn't ready to let him go.

Frank paced around in his pajamas, looking sleepy and irritated, while Bethie did her best to steady their younger brother.

"Want a beer?" Frank finally said to Emmett.

"He doesn't need a beer," Bethie said before Emmett could answer. "That's the last thing he needs."

"Christ, Bethie! Just trying to calm his nerves."

That was when she happened to look up and see us peeking through the door. "What are you boys doing up? You get right back to bed! Now!"

Her voice was so sharp and the scene in front of us so strange we obeyed immediately, scrambling back down the stairs and hopping back into bed. We were both pretending to be asleep when, a half hour later, our mother came back downstairs. I heard her tiptoeing into our room. I kept my eyes closed when she kissed me on the head and pulled up my thin summer blanket. She turned to do the same with Danny, but his curiosity was too strong for him to play possum any longer.

"What's the matter with Emmett?" he asked Bethie.

I turned over in my bed. She looked at me, sighed in a why-are-you-still-awake? sort of way, then knelt down between our two beds, touching each of us with an outstretched arm.

"Nothing's wrong. He just had a bad dream."

It seemed for a moment that that was all she was going to say, but she lingered there on the floor between us, and then after a moment spoke again.

"He was in the war," she said. "Just like Frank was. Just like your father was."

The war. People kept talking about it, or trying not to talk about it. Once again I had that image in my mind, of the dark smudge that hovered in the time before I was born, and that somehow had marked all the adults I knew.

"Were you in the war?" I asked her.

"Yes, honey, I was in the Army. But I didn't fight, I was just a nurse. But I took care of lots of people, and it's normal for those people to have bad dreams, just like Emmett had tonight. Now you two go to sleep and don't worry. Everything's just fine upstairs now. Everybody's fine. And you boys have a big day tomorrow, because you're going over to the Place."

"The Place" was what our grandfather called the Chevrolet dealership where he was general manager, and where Frank worked as a salesman. We loved going there.

"So you both go to sleep and don't worry about anything."

But I noticed, after she kissed me good night, that the tears that must have still filled her eyes had left a wet spot on my cheek.

Danny—reassured by Bethie, and excited rather than frightened by the commotion—went to sleep soon enough, but I lay there restlessly for a long time. I could hear Frank's and Emmett's voices upstairs. I couldn't make out what they were saying, just the conversational back-and-forth rhythms of two young men talking far into the night and not giving any sign that they had the intention of going back to sleep.

Looking back on it now, I'm sure that Emmett's dream that night had been brought on by the low-flying plane that had appeared so suddenly above our heads in the park, a thrill for me and Danny but for a veteran of the Italian campaign in World War II, as I later learned that Emmett had been, it could very well have been a jolting reminder of the Luftwaffe planes overhead at the invasion beaches of Salerno. He himself never said much about the war—neither to me nor to the children, my cousins, he eventually had. But not long ago we came across some pages from his service record, a sheaf of papers stuffed into a tackle box in his attic. The words I saw there— "Rapido River"—brought back the memory of a World War II documentary I had watched late one night while Jeannette was asleep beside me on the couch recovering from a savage attack of vertigo that had been a side effect of one of her chemo drugs.

Emmett would have been twenty-one or twenty-two when the 36th Division was ordered to cross this perilously cold and swift Italian river in the winter of 1944. The attack was a part of the attempt to break through the Gustav Line, the most formidable of the German army's three defensive cordons blocking the Allied advance to Rome. But it was close to a suicide mission. The approach to the river, the river itself, and the valley beyond the far bank were all under the eyes, and under the guns, of German positions on the mountain heights. The slaughter began at night, the men of the 36th torn apart by mines and mortar shells and machine-gun fire as they staggered toward the river carrying the heavy rubber boats that, once in the river itself, were likely to be capsized by the force of the current or shredded and sunk by German shrapnel. The men who made it across the river ended up being cut off from supplies or ammunition or reinforcements, in enemy territory, with no way to move forward, no boats to retreat across the river, confused and lost and alone as the mortar shells the Germans called "she-wolves" screamed down on them from the sky.

I don't know what part Emmett took in the disastrous Rapido assault—his service record doesn't say—but something about the piercing, anguished nothing-syllables I heard as he cried out on that long-ago night makes me think he might have been one of those men stranded in the dark on the wrong side of the river, a narrow river that to a young man whose friends had disappeared into its depths or were unreachable on the far bank might as well have been as wide as an ocean.

4

Our grandfather's name was Daniel, just like Danny's, and we called him Big Dan. There was nothing striking about his height—he was a little under six feet—and though he was sedentary and a bit overweight, you wouldn't have thought of him as big in the sense of taking up a lot of space. But to us he was as towering and stolid as the Biltmore Hotel downtown.

He had a steady temperament and a sense of humor that displayed itself mostly in subtle appreciation when someone else told a joke or a story. He would laugh softly then or smile almost shyly, shaking his head in mock exasperation. He had grown up in a big Irish family on a Kansas farm, but if there were any stereotypical Irish raconteurs in that family the trait wasn't passed down to him. Sometimes, after dinner, we would sit out with him on the broad porch of the main house, and people walking by on the way to the drugstore and its soda fountain at the end of the block would wave at him and he would wave back and call out to them, "What do you think of my boys here?"

In a man so taciturn, this out-of-nowhere burst of pride surprised and greatly pleased me. And sometimes Danny and I would get to take turns sleeping in the big house. On those nights when it was my turn I would start out in bed between my grandparents, laughing sleepily as Big Dan shook me by the shoulders and nuzzled his raspy unshaven face against mine, murmuring "grrr" like a benevolent monster until I finally fell asleep. In the morning I might mysteriously wake up in Vivian's bedroom, underneath her chenille bedspread, looking across the room where she sat putting on her makeup and sorting through a selection of tiny perfume bottles with rubber squeeze bulbs. "I hope you don't mind," she would tell me. "You look so cute when you're asleep I just had to steal you away."

It was Big Dan's steadiness that anchored the childhood security I felt in that sprawling household. I suppose that security was in part an illusion, a spell that all of the adults actively worked to create and maintain for the two fatherless boys who had landed in their midst. They intended to start the world anew with us, to keep us innocent of the war that in some sense had created us, had made us half-orphans.

My grandmother was very much a part of that conspiracy. She came from the same corner of Kansas as Big Dan's family, had grown up in a small farming town only a few miles away. She and Big Dan went to high school together, were married at nineteen, had the first of their five children—a girl—at twenty and lost her five years later to diphtheria. That early tragedy may have been the source of the watchfulness and fretfulness

I was always aware of in my grandmother. Or perhaps it was a legacy from the Old World, from her parents, who had forsaken their deep ancestral connections in Czechoslovakia to make a bold and frightening new start in the unknown American Midwest.

She had grown up speaking Czech, and on Sunday afternoons when she sat at the kitchen table speaking to her mother back in Kansas on her red Bakelite telephone, we would listen, amazed, as she drifted into a language of which we could not latch on to a single syllable. When she spoke that language, she seemed distant and powerful. Only a few of those alien words had ever entered our own vocabulary—one of them was the name we knew her by: Babi, a diminutive of *babička*, the Czech word for "grandmother." She had chosen her grandmother name herself, she once told me, because she didn't want to be completely cut off from the language of her own childhood. No doubt she had at one point fruitlessly tried to teach her children at least some Czech, but when the family had moved away from their little Kansas town to Oklahoma City when my mother was in high school, away from any concentrated Czech population and into a sophisticated prairie metropolis, the need to communicate in an ancient European tongue must have seemed the farthest thing from their impatient young minds.

But those incomprehensible conversations with her octogenarian mother did not mean that Babi had sealed herself into the past. She had more energy than her husband, had more of a need to be busy and connected to the society around her. Somehow in the midst of her nonstop cooking—noodle soup and goulash and kolaches and fried chicken—she was always rushing out of the house to an Altar Society or book club meeting, or was upstairs in the spare bedroom with a pair of scissors clipping newspaper articles and recipes and prayer meditations to firm up the minds or help save the souls of less industrious relatives scattered across the country.

Maybe all this activity could just be chalked up to metabolism, but I suspect that it was part of an unconscious strategy to keep her thoughts at bay, to outpace the worries and memories that threatened to catch up to her and engulf her. Among them was the death of her young daughter. She told me about this once, many years later, when I was an adult. The girl, Mary Helen, had seemed to be recovering, but then one afternoon she woke in a wild-eyed panic, called out "What's happening? What's happening?" and flung her arms out and died before anybody could do anything to calm or comfort her. Then there had been the chronic anxiety Babi must have felt during the war, when her two sons and her son-in-law were in harm's way on the ground in Europe and in the air over the Pacific, an anxiety that could not have fully abated when her boys came home safe in body but also uncommunicative and unsettled. And following the end of the war had been the aftershock of my father's death, and the emotional and logistical and financial burdens of making a home for a shattered daughter and two grandchildren.

"Stop fidgeting," Bethie told me that next morning as she wrestled me into a pair of long pants. "You know that you have to look nice when you go downtown."

Looking nice, dressing up in matching outfits, was the price we had to pay to go to the Place with Big Dan. He drove us there himself in one of the dealership's demos, a two-toned

Styleline Deluxe with a Sahara Beige body and a Regal Maroon top. As always, we rode standing up unrestrained on the bench seat beside him, and if for some reason Big Dan had to lurch to a sudden stop he would throw out his right arm in front of us, a gesture that in those days was the closest thing to a seat belt.

Chickasaw Chevrolet was on West Main, in the heart of downtown. Big Dan made a turn into an alley behind the building and rolled up in his two-toned demo car to a parking space with a sign above it that read "Daniel Brennan, General Manager." I was a precocious reader, though I don't remember whether I had actually deciphered that sign for myself or had it read to me by an adult. In any case, there was a thrill of pride whenever I saw my grandfather's name emblazoned on that concrete wall. And to walk with Big Dan through the service-and-parts department on our way to the showroom, to see the genuine warmth and respect of the Chickasaw Chevrolet employees as they said their affectionate good-mornings to him and to us, made me think that the title of General Manager carried the same charge as President of the United States.

Frank was waiting for us in the showroom, standing with the other salesmen among the gleaming floor models—the fastback sedans with their sunshades and fender skirts and rocket-shaped hood ornaments. At a time when new cars came in a broad-spectrum color palette, not just the whites and grays and silvers of today, and when the unveiling of the new models each fall was an eagerly anticipated national event, entering a showroom was like entering a shining American daydream. On the wall hung a poster that I could read for myself. It featured the singer Dinah Shore, beaming out at the viewer with the words to the song she sang on television and radio—"See the U.S.A. in Your Chevrolet"—printed in streaming letters overhead against a dark-blue, star-filled sky. She stood in front of a red convertible, wearing a ball gown, glowing with such radiant conviction about the product she was promoting that just looking at her smile made me feel happy, as if she had specifically chosen to welcome me to join her and the rest of the world in a wondrous celebration.

Big Dan took us upstairs to his office, where the wood-paneled walls were crowded with Dealer of the Year plaques. A picture window looked down onto the sales floor. He took a seat behind his desk and picked up the already ringing phone as we stood at the window. It felt strange to see our uncle Frank down there, to observe him from above and from a distance in the same way we observed the sun bear at the zoo. Several of the other salesmen were talking to customers, but Frank stood by himself at the edge of the showroom, walking in tight circles, his eyes focused through the floor-to-ceiling showroom windows on the street outside. I could sense how eager he was for a new customer to walk through the door.

While we watched Frank, we heard Big Dan on the tele-phone, his voice low and congenial but, for one flashing moment, a bit stern. From my own long experience in the same job my grandfather held, it's easy enough for me to imag-ine the cascade of issues he would have been dealing with that day and every day: the tensions that arise among department managers with different goals, all of them representing a sepa-rate profit center competing for revenue from the same bottom line; the inherent customer distrust of car dealers; the problem of finding and retaining good workers in the body shop; the never-ending inventory anxiety about the unsold vehicles and shelves of parts verging toward obsolescence.

He finally hung up the phone, then gestured with an outstretched hand to a manager who had just come through the door, signaling him to hold off a minute. When the man had made a sheepish retreat, Big Dan swiveled toward us in his office chair and said, "Now let's see—if I remember right, we got a few dealer promos in the other day."

He reached into his pocket for his keys, unlocked a deep drawer on the side of his desk, and brought out two of the plain cardboard boxes we had learned to recognize and lust after. He handed one to each of us. I opened mine and found a model Chevrolet station wagon. It was bright red and made out of die-cast metal, and had rubber wheels that could sluggishly rotate. Danny's was a black convertible.

"If either of you boys don't like what you have there," Big Dan said, "I can probably arrange a trade-in."

But we were happy enough with what we had already been given, and spent the next hour or so on the spacious floor of our grandfather's office, pushing the cars across the linoleum, racing them along an imaginary highway, enraptured as children have always been by miniature, manipulable representations of the full-scale objects that loom over our lives. Big Dan was on the phone for much of that time, or else conferring with various staff members from the dealership who popped into his office and said "Well, look what we have here!" or some other standard-issue grown-up greeting when they saw us. Then they would turn to the boss and present him with papers to look over or things to sign or problems to solve.

Frank came in as well. He made a point of admiring our toy cars and talking to us about them, but we could see that his thoughts were elsewhere and that Big Dan was subtly nervous or maybe even irritated about Frank being in his office and not down in the showroom. No doubt it's always a tricky thing, if you're a boss, to hire your own son, and even trickier if you're in charge of an operation like a car dealership, where the salesmen work on commission and are therefore always assessing who has an edge and resenting how they came to have it.

"I need to talk to you about Jerome," he told his father.

"Not right now, Frank."

Frank looked over at us. He was aware of the admonishment in Big Dan's voice, but I could also tell he was worked up and wasn't going to let go of whatever it was that was bothering him.

"He's ruining my sale. That car has been sitting on the lot, dying a slow death, for ten months. And now when I've finally got a buyer the make-ready guys say it'll be—"

"I'll talk to him. He's backed up down there."

"Or he's lazy. Dad, if I don't have that car by this afternoon—"

"I'll talk to him, Frank. I said I would. I'll talk to him and you go on back down to the floor."

Big Dan hadn't raised his voice, and his tone wasn't even particularly sharp, but a child can sense threatening discord the way an animal can detect some nameless change in the atmosphere that warns of an earthquake or an approaching tsunami. Danny and I were silent and still as Frank stood there in front of his father's desk, jingling his keys nervously in his pocket as he searched for some answer that might help him save face in front of his nephews. Finally, he just nodded his head in an angry chopping motion, said okay, and left the office.

"Keep playing with your cars," Big Dan told us as he picked up the phone again. "Then we'll go over and have lunch in a minute."

He punched one of the clear plastic buttons at the base of the phone to call his secretary, Miss Goldstein. "Wendy, see if you can locate Jerome for me, will you?"

He sat there holding the receiver to his ear for a few moments, smiling down at us without saying anything, then began speaking to the person who came onto the line. I couldn't hear the words that were said on the other end of the call but could make out the cheerful, ebullient register of the voice. We knew Jerome, the short, tautly muscled Black man in the service department who was always the first to grin at Danny and me and say hello and brag about how big we had gotten every time we visited Chickasaw Chevrolet.

"I know, I know," Big Dan was saying to him, "I understand. But I'd appreciate it, as a favor to me, if you could do whatever you could to move that car along as fast as possible."

He thanked Jerome and hung up the phone. For a long moment he seemed to have forgotten his grandchildren were in the office with him. He just sat there staring at the award plaques on the wall—staring past them with a look of irritation on his face. Then all at once the look was gone, and he clapped his hands together and said, "Let's eat!"

The Katz drugstore—the one with the sign in the shape of a cat with a bow tie—was just a block away. Big Dan held our hands as we walked down the street, under another neon sign that read "Let's Eat at Katz," and through the vast drugstore's front door. We found seats at the lunch counter, where the busy young waitresses wore white dresses and white boat-shaped caps, to my eyes no different than the nurse's uniform that my mother wore during her shift at St. Anthony's, and therefore just as gravely important to the functioning of the world. Big Dan ordered us all hamburgers, making sure not to allow mine and Danny's to be contaminated with mustard. While we waited for our lunch I stared at the Snow Crop machine a few feet down from me along the counter, a glass vessel like a water cooler in which three revolving blades stirred a pulpy slurry of orange juice. To a child with no understanding of electrical motors and no bright dividing line in his imagination between animate and inanimate things, those moving blades seemed to belong to a conscious being grimly focused on its eternal duty.

A girl stepped up to the counter next to the orange-juice machine shortly after we received our hamburgers. She was far older than me—eleven or twelve—but there was something in her demeanor that made me understand how nervous she was, and that narrowed the age difference I felt. And the fact that she was Black made her seem not just conspicuous but strikingly vulnerable.

"What is it, hon?" one of the waitresses asked her. I didn't sense any hostility in her voice, just a gentle impatience.

"My mama told me to get two chicken-salad sandwiches to go."

"Your mama here in the store somewhere?"

The girl said "Yes, ma'am" and the waitress started to write down the order on her pad. A man sitting on a counter stool next to the one the girl was standing beside stared at her. He was in his thirties, wearing a suit, his gray hat with its black hatband resting on the counter next to his lunch plate. He took a bite of his sandwich and said in a flat tone to the waitress, "She's not supposed to be here."

"She can't sit, but she can order something to go. So that's what she's doing. You just wait here, hon, and I'll get your order."

The waitress disappeared and the man kept staring at the girl. "Don't you sit on that stool," he told her. "I'm watching you." She had no intention of taking a seat. Oklahoma City was half a decade or more away from the organized sit-ins that would liberate its lunch counters and restaurants. She just stared straight ahead, then turned her head to the back of the store, hoping to find her mother. I could see how afraid she was of the man; she was trembling. The man also saw this, and it seemed to please and embolden him. He spoke to her again: "You just keep your little nigger behind right where it is."

The word wasn't unknown to me; of course it wasn't. I had heard Frank or Emmett use it in jokes, I had heard it from other kids. But I had never heard the word addressed, with such vicious matter-of-factness, to a human being. I had never seen it register on the frozen face of a terrified girl.

A voice I didn't recognize at first said, "Hey!" The single word came from the person on the stool next to mine. It traveled like a bullet down the counter, past me, past the girl, aimed at the man who had interrupted his lunch to torment her. "Hey!" was all my grandfather said. He didn't follow it up with any statement or further admonishment, but his voice was loud enough to pierce the background noise of lunchroom conversation and clattering plates and the sound of the hamburger patties hissing on the grill. And it was level and confident enough to be perceived as a challenge that could be backed up.

But there was no confrontation. The man gave a snorty little laugh in response and went back to his lunch without saying anything else. The waitress brought the chicken-salad sandwiches in a white bag; the girl put some money down on the counter and fled to the interior of the drugstore in search of her mother. Big Dan and Danny and I finished our lunch and then Big Dan drove us home before he went back to work.

I don't want to claim too much for my grandfather. He was a car dealer, a white businessman who, at least in my hearing, never offered an opinion one way or another about the foundation of exclusion and inequity that supported our existence in 1950s Oklahoma City. I wouldn't be surprised to learn that the chastening word he barked at the Katz lunch counter that day had more to do with an expectation of civil behavior than any real concern for social justice. Back then I couldn't have known enough to begin to make that distinction. But I remember being aware at that moment of a new sensation, a power I hadn't known about before now, the power to declare myself to myself. I even remember, at five years old, watching Big Dan take a bite of his hamburger as if nothing had just happened, and forming the words in my mind: "That's how I want to be."

5

"What did you boys think of Hugh?" Vivian asked as she walked with Danny and me after dinner to the end of the block.

"Who's Hugh?" Danny said. He had already forgotten, or hadn't bothered to notice, the name of the mysterious man who had showed up at the park that evening of the balloon drop. Danny was a whole year older than I was, and therefore, it seemed to me, that much more daring and confident. A part of me innocently believed that when I was six like my brother I would be as fearless as he was, but there was another part that recognized that our natures were different and that we would stay that way through life. Like our mother, I would always be on the alert for things to worry about, anticipating even as I was falling asleep the nightmares that were shuffling forward to arrive. But Danny, in appearance and in outlook, would be as bold and incautious as our dead hero father.

That was probably the reason he didn't recognize Hugh's name when Vivian asked us about him. Unlike me, he wasn't habitually on the lookout for ominous developments. But for me there had been something about the arrival of this stranger that created a quaver in the air, that felt like, not a threat, not an assault, but some sort of intrusion whose significance I had no way of gauging.

"He was that man we saw in the park," I said.

"That's right, Grady. Didn't you two think he was nice?"

All we could think of to do in response to this unusual question was to shrug.

"Well, *I* think he's very nice," Vivian said. She told us Hugh lived in Texas, that he had something to do with oil, but that his mother lived in Oklahoma City and he came back to see her often.

"I approve of men who are good to their mothers," she said. "That's also one of the reasons I approve of my handsome little nephews. And I think I'm going to buy them each a double scoop."

The drugstore at the corner of our street was a much humbler place than Katz's, but like all such enterprises back then it had a soda fountain. Vivian bought us ice-cream cones at the counter and we walked outside and sat on a bench facing Classen Boulevard.

"Sometimes I just like to sit here and watch the cars go by," Vivian said.

There were a lot of cars to watch. Classen was a busy street, and after a while the three of us seemed to fall into a bewitched reverie, lulled by the street noise and by the way the cars, in the twilight that was just now coming on, seemed to be locked into secret errands of their own that had nothing to do with the drivers and passengers inside them.

"And lord knows your mother deserves a chance to be

happy again," Vivian said, out of the blue, after a long spell of silence.

"She's not happy?" Danny asked.

"Well, of course she is. How could she not be happy with you two little munchkins? What would any of us do without you boys? I just meant . . . Hey, would you like to see a picture?"

She handed her half-finished ice-cream cone to me while she opened her beaded handbag, took out her pocketbook, snapped it open, and paged through the clear plastic photo sleeves until she found the snapshot she was looking for. Then she held it in front of us so that we could see.

"That was taken before either of you was even a gleam in anybody's eye."

It was a picture I had never seen before. It showed our mother and our father—the ghost we knew as Burt—sitting at a table at a nightclub or a restaurant. They were holding hands on top of the table. They were both in uniform, Burt hatless, Bethie wearing a billed Army cap from which her brown hair cascaded down in waves. Burt's smile was so broad that it traveled up his face and closed his eyes, but my mother's eyes—her familiar brown eyes—were open, gazing at the camera with a contentment and serenity that left me off-balance. For the first time I had the understanding that once upon a time my father had been real. And I sensed the magnitude of what had happened to my mother, what had been taken away from her.

"Who do you think he looks like?" Vivian asked us. "I think he has your mouth, Danny, don't you? And there's something around the eyes—something I can't quite put my finger on—that I can see in you, Grady. But look at your mother! Isn't she gorgeous? Isn't she just beaming? That's the way I want to see her again."

I had never seen Vivian cry before, and I didn't exactly see it now. She didn't sniffle or wipe away tears. She just stared at the photo for a moment longer before snapping her pocketbook shut again and then smiled at Danny and me in a way we didn't anticipate, a smile whose purpose seemed to be to ward off some other, stronger emotion.

We finished our ice cream on the way home, walking down the sidewalk under the sycamore branches that lined the street, night falling and the shushing sound of the Classen traffic fading into the background.

Then we came into the range of a familiar voice. We were a few houses away from our grandparents' house when I heard Frank's hurt, haranguing tone. He was arguing heatedly about something. As we got closer, I could see him and Big Dan on the porch. Frank was in motion, pacing back and forth in front of a square brick column. My grandfather sat across from him on a porch glider, tight-lipped, not saying anything. I could make out only snatches of Frank's angry lecture—"Oh, so I guess you think it's easy being the boss's son? . . . How much notice does Jerome really need to make a car ready, for Christ's sake? . . . You wouldn't put up with that kind of behavior from a white man, I don't see why you do with a—"

Big Dan cut him off with a wave of his hand as he caught sight of Vivian and Danny and me walking up to the house. "Well, hello there," he called out to us as he stood up from his porch swing. "Don't believe I've seen you folks before. New to the neighborhood?"

Frank made a point of smiling at us also, though his overall expression was rigid. I understood that he was impatient to get back to his argumentative train of thought, back to the fight with his father. In trying to recall and record here some fragments of their conversation I might be leaving an impression I had some idea what they were fighting about. But I didn't. I was a child, and was only aware of the cold threat that a child feels when the atmosphere around him turns confusing, when the people he assumes to be exclusively concerned with his welfare and happiness suddenly shift their attention away and wander off into some oppressive gray space where he is neither equipped nor allowed to follow.

"If you can pull yourselves away from whatever urgent topic you're discussing," Vivian said to her father and brother, "you might want to say good night to Danny and Grady before I deliver them to their mother."

Big Dan came down the porch stairs and lifted Danny and me in turn, making an animal sound as he squeezed us against his chest and rubbed his chin against the tops of our heads. Frank was still distracted. He stayed on the porch and muttered "Sleep tight, boys" as Vivian—with a disapproving glance back at her brother—led us around the side of the house and up the driveway to our apartment in back.

Our mother gave us a bath, put us into our summer pajamas, then sat with us on the maroon velvet couch and read to us as she did every night. We had advanced beyond Little Golden Books, with their simple illustrations of kittens and puppies and anthropomorphic dump trucks, and their unthreatening blocks of wide-spaced text—words that I knew so well by heart, from the shape of their letters and the sound of my mother's soft enunciation, that I had learned to read without realizing it.

But now we were on to the strange and ungraspable literature found in a series of children's books called My Book House, a multivolume set that was sold door-to-door in those days like encyclopedias and that had been bought for us by our grandparents after our father was killed and they knew that our broken family would be coming to live with them. The books had titles—*Through the Gate, Over the Hills, Through Fairy Halls, From the Tower Window*—that conjured up for me a succession of haunted journeys, of setting forth into mildly forbidding worlds from which there was no guarantee of a safe return.

Tonight's volume was *Up One Pair of Stairs*. Like the other books in the series, it was a compendium of Old World folk tales, Bible stories, and Victorian English verse. "There were three jovial Welshmen," Bethie read as she held the book in her lap and we hitched closer to her, feeling drowsy from the bath and her body heat and the sound of her voice. "As I have heard them say / And they would go a-hunting / Upon St. David's Day."

I still have that book, the sole remnant of my childhood library, the survivor of many moves and of many decades in attics and in rented storage units. The fact that it hasn't managed to disappear from my life is the reason I'm able to set down here the verses from such an obscure and long-forgotten poem. The book has splotchy, mildewed pages and smells like it was just retrieved from a buried time capsule. But I remember how ancient the book seemed to me even when it was new, with its art-nouveau illustrations and its references to things— like dormice and woodsmen and mock turtles—that meant nothing in the Oklahoma universe we inhabited. What was a jovial Welshman? What was St. David's Day? It didn't matter. There was a kind of comfort in not knowing, in not asking, in trusting that I needn't be troubled because my mother knew the answers to these and all other secrets.

I went to sleep that night listening to Danny, on the other side of our narrow bedroom, run the toy car that Big Dan had given him that morning up and down along the wall behind his bed. When I woke up an hour or two later, Danny was asleep, the car on the floor beside him. I got out of bed, not scared this time, just aware that something about the atmosphere of our apartment was different.

When I walked into the living room I saw what had changed. Emmett was there, sitting at a card table in the middle of the room. His head was bent over and he was oblivious to the world around him as he made crosshatching motions on a piece of paper with a colored pencil. It was not just the unexpected presence of Emmett that surprised me. It was also the new configuration of the room—the card table, which my mother usually kept folded up and stored away behind the sofa, and the glare of the portable lamp that Emmett had clamped to its side. He didn't notice me standing there in my pajamas watching him, and he was so focused on what he was doing he didn't look like he ever would. In that harsh lamplight my uncle, still in his twenties, looked like an old man—his eyes narrowed, his lips compressed, the white skin of his starkly illuminated forehead contrasting with his black hair. I don't know how long I stood there watching him before my presence startled him out of his concentration.

"What are you doing up, Grady?" he asked, his voice mild and his face friendly and youthful again. "You're supposed to be in there sawing logs."

I had no idea what he was talking about. The phrase "sawing logs" produced a mental flash of something like those nauseatingly wiggly cartoon characters we watched on TV, in this case a humanoid beaver buzzing through a forest, gnawing through the trees at breathtaking speed.

"Where's my mother?" I asked Emmett.

"Oh, she went out for a little while," he said cheerily. "She and Vivian are double-dating. Know what a double date is?"

"No."

"You will—in another, say, ten or eleven years. Anyway, I'm on duty till she gets back. Want to see what I'm drawing?"

I walked closer and he reached out and lifted me into his lap. On the table was an almost finished color sketch of the Lone Ranger, mounted on Silver, his white stallion. The horse reared up beside a towering jumble of rocks just like he did on the opening credits of the show we watched on the small television set at the other end of the room. The pencil sketch was strikingly accurate, mysteriously real. There was the Lone Ranger in his white hat, his black mask, his bandanna, his spangled gun belt and holster. It was even more riveting than the screen version, since it was in color. I had only seen the Lone Ranger's skintight cowboy costume on black-and-white television, but in Emmett's color-pencil rendering it was a mind-expanding bright blue.

Emmett worked as a draftsman for a land survey company downtown. We had never been to his office, but he had once driven us by the building where he worked and pointed to a row of upper windows that he said was the location of Miss Esmerelda's Home for Disappointed Artists.

It was a sardonic joke that was, of course, pitched far above our comprehension. But I was aware, however fuzzily, of the truth behind it. I don't know exactly what sort of future Emmett had envisioned for himself, but he had a wistful, halfway-defeated quality that a confused child like me could recognize and identify with. I know now what I didn't know then, and would have been too young, even if I had known, to appreciate. After the war, he had spent a few years stuck in place with anxiety and depression before picking up his life again and enrolling at the University of Oklahoma to study art. But he had been there only a few semesters when my father was killed. His response was to withdraw from school, move home from Norman, and move into the garage apartment with Frank. Bethie had begged him not to back away from his future like that, but he wouldn't listen. He convinced himself that his sister and her two boys needed him more than he needed a college degree, more than the world needed another artist.

Would he have been a visionary painter or sculptor? I don't know, but to my eyes his rendering of the Lone Ranger that night was a miracle. I sat in his lap, growing sleepy again. As he finished the sketch, the cowboy figure and his horse became even more inscrutably vibrant.

"It's for you and Danny," he said. "Here, look, it's even signed by the artist. Should we display it for the public?"

He stood up, found a blank space on the wood-paneled wall next to the television, and affixed the drawing to it with a thumbtack. We stood back and admired it for a minute or two before he picked me up and carried me back to my bed.

I went back to sleep, but it couldn't have been for long. I woke to the lowered voices of my mother and Emmett. The door to our bedroom was open. I climbed out of bed, hid behind the doorframe, and peered into the living room. Emmett still sat in the chair where he had been sketching at the card table. Bethie was on the couch, dressed for the evening out she had just come home from, her face made up. But her face was streaked with tears, and the sight of that—combined with a faint but unfamiliar trace of perfume—drove me away from the door and back into my bed. I didn't want my mother to be sad, and I didn't want her to be strange.

But I lay in bed and kept listening, even if I was too unsettled to continue to be an eyewitness, an observer of the sorrow on Bethie's face.

"Of course I *like* him," she was telling Emmett. "He's thoughtful, he's kind, he's interesting, everything Vivian kept telling me he would be. It's not him . . . it's . . . Burt." She said the name of her husband, our dead father, with a shuddering wail that startled me, that pressed me down in my bed. The sound lasted only for a moment; she stifled herself into silence before another involuntary eruption of grief could escape from her body.

"The door," she said, "the boys . . ."

And I heard Emmett rise from his chair and saw him softly close the door to our bedroom, shutting out the light from the living room and stranding me in a darkness relieved only by the Hopalong Cassidy night-light. Their voices were more muted now, but I could still hear. They kept on talking about Hugh, the man in the park, the man she had been on a "double date" with.

"What if I end up really liking him?" she asked Emmett. "What happens then? What happens if I marry him?"

"What's wrong with that?"

"He doesn't live here. He lives in Texas. He'd want us to move there. How can I take the boys away from you and Frank and Vivian and Mother and Daddy? What would that do to them? Especially Grady."

Especially me? I didn't know what she meant. What was different about me? Was it the fact that I was worried and awake when my older brother was sound asleep in the bed next to mine? But then I didn't know what she meant about anything. "Take the boys away" was a menacing phrase that conjured up an image of my mother fleeing with us in our pajamas down the driveway in the middle of the night while my grandparents ran after us, crying out in sorrow and betrayal.

I don't know how long Bethie and Emmett talked—how long my uncle comforted my mother in the same way that she, a few nights before, had comforted him. Because despite my fretful incomprehension I managed to fall asleep.

Bethie woke us up in the morning as usual and got us dressed. The card table in the living room had been put away, the lamp carried back upstairs to Emmett's drafting table. But the picture of the Lone Ranger was still pinned to the wall, and we stared at it as we ate our breakfast. Perhaps because it was in color, perhaps because there was some artistry in the sketch that we could experience but not recognize, the Lone Ranger on the wall seemed more alive than the one that appeared on our tiny television screen.

"Your uncle is a real Michelangelo, isn't he?" Bethie said as she walked out of her bedroom in her nurse's uniform. She was far more lighthearted than she had been in the middle of the night, and I wondered if her sobbing on the couch with Emmett was just something I had dreamed.

"And guess what? I have a surprise for you two."

She reached into the twin front pockets of her uniform dress and brought out two small red plastic motorcycles.

Seated on each motorcycle was a blue policeman, not fused to the vehicle as was the case with inferior and less interesting toys, but detachable, capable of being snapped on and off with a satisfying click.

"Do you know who those are from? They're from Hugh. Remember that nice man we met in the park? He wanted you to have them. Wasn't that thoughtful?"

I wasn't aware enough to question this gift, to suspect that a stranger interested in our mother might have given it to us as a means of buying favor with her children. In any case I would have been too pleased to care. In addition to the toy promo car from my grandfather, I had a new police motorcycle, bestowed upon me by a mysterious man that people kept talking about without quite telling us who he was or why he was so important, or the changes he might bring to a family that I naively believed to be already complete.

6

Someone must have been keeping an eye on us. Some adult must have been discreetly watching from a distance, or at least glancing our way from time to time from a window or over a hedge. But maybe not. Maybe Danny and I were as at-large and unsupervised as it appeared to us as we roamed through the vast-seeming park that was effectively our backyard.

The fountain at the far end of the park, the memorial to the dead of World War I, was a four-tiered structure, each tier a shallow basin that, when the fountain was turned on, would catch the overflowing water from the smaller-diameter tier above, creating a broadening waterfall. But the fountain was rarely in operation. Most of the time it just sat there, a series of stucco circles like a giant stack of pancakes rising from a dried-up reflecting pool.

Sometimes older kids would lug a few of the green wooden benches that were scattered around the park to the base of the fountain and set them on end. They would use the first upended bench as a rickety ladder to climb to the lowest tier, then haul another bench up and repeat the process until they stood triumphantly and dangerously on top, at the highest and narrowest of the concentric circles, thirty-five or forty feet into the air.

There were no older kids at the fountain today. Since the water was off as usual, and some of the benches were around, Danny determined we should climb to the top, all by ourselves. We dragged a bench down into the empty reflecting pool, somehow manhandled it until it was standing on end, the top end resting on the lip of the first and broadest basin of the fountain. It was only a few feet above our heads but to my eyes it looked as distant as a mountain summit. I watched in alarm as Danny scrambled up the upturned bench and disappeared over the broad edge of the basin. Then his face was visible again, staring impatiently down at me and ordering "C'mon!"

There was no obvious way to climb a park bench that had been set on end. The horizontal wooden slats that made up its seat now ran vertically, so there were no spaces between them where I could wedge a toe. I had to grip hard on the back of the bench with both hands and haul myself up while my feet kept skidding, searching for some kind of purchase against the slats. Even though Danny held it as steady as he could from the top, the whole bench shook and teetered as I climbed.

I finally clawed my way up to the top of the bench and over the smooth stucco edge of the first tier. I found myself sitting in a broad shallow platter that, even though the fountain wasn't running, was still wet and slippery with algae and muddy leaves. I looked over the edge, to the bottom of the dry reflecting pool, which seemed to be hundreds of feet below us.

"Pull it up," Danny ordered, and we grabbed the handrails of the bench and managed to haul it up to where we were sitting. Staring at the empty air below, I didn't like the idea that we had just taken up our only way to get back down. But Danny was older, and his nature was as heedless as mine was cautious. While I was wondering how we were going to get down, he was concerned only with climbing higher. He just laughed when I nervously told him I thought we had gone high enough. All by himself, he was already settling the bench against the edge of the basin above us, and before I could protest he had already climbed up to it.

He commanded me once again to follow him. It was only the fear of being left alone that gave me the nerve to do so. It was one thing to climb up that shifting bench from ground level, it was another to do so from the midair platform on which we now stood. And when I finally made it to the next basin, which was so much smaller in diameter and so much higher off the ground that it might as well have been an eagle's nest, whatever courage I had evaporated.

"I want to go down," I told Danny.

"No," he said, "we're going all the way to the top."

He pointed upward, toward the next tier of the fountain, under which we were standing. Above it, I knew, was the last tier in this series of increasingly smaller platforms. He was already dragging the bench into position, but because the circle where we stood was narrower than the circle below it had been, there wasn't as much maneuvering room.

"Help me," he said. "Grab that end."

"No, I want to go down."

I was trembling with foreboding by that point. I shook my head in violent protest. Danny looked at me with disgust, but maybe by that time even he was questioning the wisdom of going farther. It was already a long way to the ground, and the higher we went, the chances of a serious fall off that unsteady bench ladder were obviously growing stronger. And Danny, for all his bravado, was only six years old.

He mimicked my frightened look and called me a coward, but he didn't object strongly enough to make me think I really was one. He was my big brother. He knew even when he was tormenting me that I depended on his protection and craved his respect.

So he agreed to go down. It was even scarier to descend, but at least now Danny didn't goad me the way he had done on the way up. We worked together, stage by stage, lowering the bench, shimmying precariously down the two levels we had climbed until we were finally back on the solid surface of the dry reflecting pool.

We had brought the toy motorcycles that Hugh had given us in the pockets of our short pants, and after we had left the fountain and made a circuit of our other regular stations in the park—the Shakespeare monument, the solitary sandstone boulder into which kids carved their names with sharp flakes of rock—we came to what was usually our last stop, a sandbox that sat at the bottom of the slope behind our apartment and that was visible through our kitchen window. It was a big structure, seven or eight feet square, and the sand in it was deep.

Danny busied himself outside the sandbox with an engineering project, gathering rocks and twigs and scooping up dirt to build a ramp down which he could send his motorcycle crashing. I was glad that he was preoccupied, because nothing could have contented me more than to sit in the sandbox with my own plastic motorcycle, snapping the policeman on and off the bike, studying his molded, impassive features and trying to deduce from his face and posture who he was and who he was in pursuit of.

I'm sure there's a huge body of scholarship about the meaning of toys, about the ceaseless craving that children have to handle these objects and to imagine the life that might somehow exist within them. I'm pretty old now, and my memories of that magically intimate connection with inanimate things are faded. But they're not gone. And they flare up every time I see my young grandchildren—two and three years old—enter our house and head straight for the wicker toy chest where we keep a random collection of cars with Duplo chassis and plastic squeeze toys and Mr. Potato Head parts. Those children's need to hold things in their hands, to manipulate them, and to ponder how they fit into the larger space around them seems to me like a greater need than food or water.

For me it was the human figures that inflamed my imagination the most. The way a plastic cowboy wielded his six-shooter or a soldier held his rifle suggested to me a character deeper and richer than any I had ever encountered on a movie or TV screen. They were real to me, all the more alive somehow because they were so static and stiff. Unlike the action figures of future generations, with their bendable waists and articulated limbs, they couldn't be posed or their bodies reconfigured. You had to take them on their own terms, to discover the identity hidden in their unmoving forms. A cowboy on his horse galloped sometimes across the rugged landscape of my own body, up and down my arms, through the plain of my open palm, across the boulders and canyons formed by my knuckles. In a bunched-up bedspread there were endless crevices and mountains for him to explore, and from which he could be ambushed by other figures in whose fused plastic expressions or rigid body language I sensed something sinister.

There was no greater landscape than the sandbox. It was easy to imagine a whole world spread out before my motorcycle-riding policeman, a world of endless dunes through which—I judged by the grim, fixed expression on his blue face—he was destined to ride. I was pushing his motorcycle through one of these dunes when Danny suddenly grabbed it and shoved it deep into the sand on the other side of the sandbox.

"Bet you can't find it!" he said. I knew instinctively he had decided to torment me for losing my nerve—and causing him to lose his—when we were halfway up the fountain.

"Give it back!"

"Sorry, I don't know where it is," he said, as he shoveled his hands deep into the sand, stirring it up so thoroughly that there was now no way that the place he had buried it was the place where it still was. "You have to find it."

I pawed away at the sand, frantic to find the hidden motorcycle and its rider, unable to understand how it could be so thoroughly gone. I was angry at Danny but no angrier than a younger brother had a right to be. I knew it was his business to taunt me and torture me, just as it was his business when necessary—when we were under attack from neighbor kids—to come to my defense. The stronger emotion I felt was a harrowing frustration. I knew that the motorcycle was somewhere very near, but the more I searched for it, the surer I was becoming that I would never find it, that it had disappeared from the face of the earth.

But then in an instant even that gnawing concern vanished.

I heard my mother call our names and looked up to see her running down the slope that led from our garage apartment— really running, in her white nurse's shoes. By the way her arms were extended, by the way her features had turned pale and blank, I knew that she was racing to save us from a threat we had not yet seen.

7

"Come with me right now, both of you!" Bethie said when she reached us. She grabbed us each by the hand and pulled us away from the sandbox. We wanted to know why, what was wrong, but she was in too big a hurry and too focused a frame of mind to say anything other than "I'll tell you in a minute."

I tried to pull away from her, wailing that my motorcycle was buried somewhere in the sandbox and that I had to find it. "We'll find it later!" she snapped, squeezing down so hard on my hand that I made a show of crying out in pain. My indignation didn't slow her down. The more I balked, the harder she yanked me forward. I watched her head turning anxiously from side to side as she surveyed the open parkland around us.

Things only got more confusing as we approached the gate that led from the park to our driveway. Our grandmother—Babi—was standing there in her housedress and cat's-eye glasses, looking just as vigilant as Bethie, and with a long-handled garden rake in her hands. The way she held the rake made me understand she intended to use it as a weapon, and as Bethie led us through the gate Babi lingered behind a few steps, covering our retreat.

We were hurried past our apartment and the strip of lawn in front, and through the back door of our grandparents' house. It was mid-afternoon on a Friday. The house was empty. Our mother had just gotten home from her nursing shift, but everyone besides her and Babi was still at work. Just as Bethie closed the back door I could hear the voice of a radio announcer: ". . . will attack anything and is a known man-eater, so parents of small children should immediately—"

Before we could hear more Babi hurried into the kitchen and turned off the radio, which sat on a shelf above the stove.

"What's going on? What's wrong?" Danny said.

"Nothing's wrong," Bethie answered. Her voice was calm now that we were safe in the house with her. "We just all have to stay inside for a little bit."

"Why?"

"Because . . ." She glanced at her mother before going on, trying to determine how much to tell us. I saw Babi shrug in a way that said, "They might as well know."

"Because an animal—a leopard—escaped from the zoo. And it's all right—it's all right, I promise. They're going to find him and put him back in his cage, but for now we don't want to go outside."

Her words might not have been frightening if they had been spoken in a voice that was naturally calm. But I could see that Bethie was trying too hard to project an illusion of normalcy. Even as she smiled at us and pretended that nothing was wrong, she was transmitting the fear that was coursing through her own body, and that was evident in the way she was still catching her breath after the frantic sprint we had made from the park to the safety of the house.

Her reaction was overwrought, but it wasn't all that out of sync with the reaction of the whole city during the days that the leopard was on the loose and assumed to be hungry, prowling from yard to yard and tree to tree searching for human prey. And to be fair, any mother would have panicked to some degree to hear on the radio that a man-eating cat was on the loose in her city and to know that her young children were sitting exposed in a sandbox in the middle of an open park.

Babi was cooking noodle soup. The smell of the beef bones and onions and celery simmering together in the stove's soup well filled the kitchen with a comforting familiarity. In the dining room the long sheets of noodles she had rolled out and would soon cut by hand before dropping them into the broth were draped over the chairbacks to dry.

Bethie told us that as long as we had to stay inside we could watch television, so we sat down on the living-room carpet in front of the tiny Magnavox screen. As I waited for the set to warm up, for the black-and-white images to coalesce from a field of grayish green, I thought of the toy motorcycle and its rider left behind in the sandbox, buried and vanished—not just from my sight but maybe even from the whole newly disoriented world.

After a few moments we saw the face of 3-D Danny, the host of the afternoon children's show who, because he shared a name with my brother, always seemed to me to have a secret connection to our family. He was an intimate household presence, even though he was from the far future and wore a space suit and was always manipulating the controls of a giant computing machine with blinking lights. This afternoon a mysterious "space girl" had wandered into 3-D Danny's Universal Science Corps headquarters. She wore a cape and an exotic helmet and her face was hidden by a veil. She said she couldn't remember her name or even what planet she came from. "I've got an idea!" 3-D Danny said, after he and his robot friend had wrestled with this problem for a while. "Maybe the boys and girls out there from the planet Earth can help us guess her name. All right, boys and girls, when I tell you to—"

At that moment the image of 3-D Danny disappeared and was replaced by a somber-looking local newsman sitting behind a desk. "This is an important news update for the Oklahoma City area," he announced. "The leopard that escaped from the zoo this afternoon is still at large. Residents are advised to stay in their houses with the doors closed, and to make sure your children are with you. Do not let them outside while this dangerous animal is loose."

As the announcer talked, a sketch of a leopard filled the screen. The people at the TV station, in those primitive broadcasting days long before there was such a thing as live remote reporting, had probably been scrambling to find an image they could present to the public. The sketch they put up, in black-and-white of course, showed a big spotted cat lounging in the upper branches of a tree with its legs dangling down. It could not have seemed less threatening. But then almost immediately it was switched out with an actual photograph, this one a close-up of a leopard's snarling face. Its mouth was wide open, so that its four daggerlike canine teeth were bared and the muscles above contracted, which made the cat's eyes viciously narrow. I remember jumping back a little when I saw it, though the photograph was blurry and the black-and-white screen was barely the size of a piece of tablet paper.

The photograph of the leopard startled me even more than the real thing had when I had seen it try to leap out of the pit at the zoo. This was the face of a real predator. It had burst through the comforting futuristic reveries of 3-D Danny to fix its eyes on mine and send a message that it was coming after *me*.

I know now that the escaped animal was from India, a member of one of the nine subspecies of the leopard family. Indian leopards are slightly smaller, slightly darker than African leopards. But as with all leopards, their fur is patterned with the bewitching, closely spaced black splotches called rosettes that help camouflage them in the dappled shade of the forests and grasslands where they hunt. And like all leopards they are fast and agile, with a fluid strength when it comes to climbing trees, and able to leap as far as twenty feet in one bound.

The leopard that escaped had used that lunging ability to spectacular effect. According to the newspaper accounts I dredged up, a half dozen boys—twelve and thirteen years old—were standing at the top of the pit looking down just as Danny and I had been when the two-hundred-pound creature accomplished what it hadn't when we were there: made it to the top of the rail fence to the astonishment of the boys, who all went running off in a panic. The leopard perched there above the pit for a long time, four or five minutes, looking around, and then slid off into the brush.

It hadn't been a direct leap—the pit was too deep for that. But after trying incessantly to make a frontal escape, the leopard had finally learned that if he could launch himself as high as he could go toward the wall on the side of the enclosure, he could then use the zigzag momentum he created to carry him up and out, all the way to the fence. "In billiards," the newspaper reporter wrote, "it's called a cushion shot."

Of course, I knew nothing of the details then. All I knew was that a savage animal was loose, and that moments ago I had been sitting in that sandbox in the park, preoccupied with finding my missing toy motorcycle, and as vulnerable as any unsuspecting prey on the savannah.

The snarling leopard was on the screen for a few more moments, and then we saw the newsman again, this time joined by a grim-looking bullet-headed man in an open-collared shirt without a jacket. He was sweating as if he had just been sprinting toward the TV station, which he probably had been. The newsman introduced him as a noted Oklahoma City hunter who had shot big cats on every continent and was an expert on the behavior of the leopard, the most cunning and ruthless big cat of all.

"Lions and tigers are dangerous, no doubt about it, but they kill only for food. The leopard, on the other hand, will kill for pleasure. He will hide in the trees, waiting for nighttime. And then, when darkness begins to fall, he will climb down to hunt. He is very patient. He moves without a sound. You might not know he is there—up in the trees, or on the ground—watching you, but he is. And when he strikes you will have no warning. He will—"

Bethie, who had been talking to Babi in the kitchen, rushed into the room when she heard what was being said on the television and switched it off.

"You don't need to hear any more of that," she said. "I told you there's nothing at all to worry about. They've probably already caught him by now, and if not he's bound to be miles and miles away from here."

But there was still that faint breathiness in her voice that gave me the impression that while trying to calm us she still wasn't completely calm herself. With no picture on the television set, I shifted my attention to the window behind it, which looked out past the roomy porch of our grandparents' house to the street. There was something strange going on there, a procession of cars and pickup trucks filled with people calling out to one another through their open windows in scary, exuberant voices. Riding in the bed of one of the pickup trucks were five or six men in hats and khaki pants holding rifles and drinking beer from cans. The driver of the truck honked at the car in front of him, and the driver of the car honked back, creating an echoing pandemonium all up and down NW 34th Street.

"Oh, for goodness sake!" my mother said.

"What are they doing?" I asked her.

"Oh, honey, don't worry about them. They're just acting silly. They think they're hunting the leopard."

They didn't appear to be acting silly to me. Despite all the noise they were making, they seemed in the grip of some serious, lethal excitement that was in keeping with our frantic rescue from the park, the warnings on the radio and TV for parents to keep their children indoors, and that ferocious leopard face that may have disappeared from the screen but certainly not from my thoughts. I knew, despite Bethie's attempts to make the afternoon seem normal, that a monster was on the loose.

8

"People are going crazy downtown," Vivian said when she breezed through the back door late that afternoon, home from work. "Can you imagine? The whole city is on a leopard hunt!"

My mother and Danny and I were still sequestered in our grandparents' house—mostly, I think, because Bethie was still superstitiously wary of crossing the open space between the main house and our apartment with two young children who could be snatched from her grasp by a leopard's claws. The contrast in mood between her and her younger sister was stark. Vivian was titillated by the idea of a killer cat on the loose, and even more so by the stir its escape had created in the midst of a routine day at the office.

Her sense of harmless excitement was contagious, rescuing me for a while from the fear that had been oppressing me all afternoon, and from my mother's high-alert protectiveness that had instilled that fear. I understand now, in a way I couldn't then, how Vivian could be so blithe and unconcerned when my mother hadn't yet shaken off the panic of hearing about the leopard and realizing her children were alone and vulnerable in the park.

Part of it had to do with the fact that, as close as Vivian was to Danny and me, she didn't have children of her own and so was a degree removed from the hollowed-out sensation of bodily dread that had seized our mother. And though she wasn't untouched by the war—there had, after all, been the consuming worry about her two brothers fighting overseas and the sudden death of her brother-in-law—it had been more of a background pageant in her life, nothing that she had been forced to face too directly. She had been a high-school student with a busy social life, not an Army nurse like her older sister, who was stationed at bases on the West Coast, where she would wait on the tarmac for hideously wounded men to arrive from the battles of the Pacific war, and then work endless hours in operating rooms, trying to avoid passing out from the stench of burned flesh or shredded intestines while impatient and overworked Army doctors barked at her to hand them the surgical instruments they needed and screamed at her if she made a mistake.

And more than any of that, Vivian didn't know what it was like to be a young wife and mother with the war finally behind her, with a new baby on the way and a bright new future ahead; to be watering the lawn one beautiful spring day in Washington State, smiling at her one-year-old son as he toddled across the grass; and then to see a staff car from the nearby Air Force base pull up at the curb, and to feel herself freeze solid as the doors opened and a notification team in dress uniforms, accompanied by a chaplain, stepped out and walked slowly toward her with solemnity in their eyes and with the cold-blooded forward momentum of stalking animals.

My mother's nerves had never quite settled from that moment, from being assaulted by the news of my father's death; they never would. It would be many years before I could truly grasp the fact that she lived in a constant mental climate of foreboding, aware in a still-raw way that the potential for sudden death lurked everywhere.

So it was natural she would interrupt her chattering sister and tell her, "It's not a joke, Vivian."

"Well, of course it's not a joke," Vivian said. We were all in the kitchen now, and Vivian was looking approvingly over her mother's shoulder as Babi dropped handfuls of homemade noodles into the broth simmering in the soup well. "But come on, Bethie, the zoo is a long way away from here."

"Only six miles," Babi said as she stirred the soup. "That's close enough for me."

"Is the leopard going to get us?" I remember the quaking tone of voice in which I uttered those words, the way the uncomprehending fear I had been holding inside all afternoon came flooding through me, bursting out of me, my eyes suddenly manufacturing tears that felt as big as raindrops against my cheeks.

All at once the three women in the kitchen descended upon me, Bethie and Vivian on their knees looking earnestly into my eyes, Babi hovering above me with her hand on my head—all of them whispering urgent soothing words, wiping away my tears, promising nothing and no one was ever going to hurt me.

Danny called me a crybaby but Bethie turned to him and

said, "Hush! Don't ever say that about your brother!" The humiliation I might have normally felt at my older brother's contempt was eclipsed by this welcome surge of female attention.

"What's the matter here?" Big Dan said when he came home through the back door and saw me sobbing in the kitchen.

"Grady's afraid of the leopard," Danny told him. Now that another male had entered the room, he didn't try to hide the mockery in his voice.

"Well, there's no reason to be afraid," he said. "That poor leopard's probably more scared than anybody else. I bet right now he's trying to find his way back to his cage."

He walked into the living room and sat down in his chair, the chair with a beanbag ashtray always resting on one arm. I felt the attention of my mother and aunt and grandmother shift away from me and toward him. I resented it, but even in my childish distress I had caught the odd tone in his voice when he offered me his reassuring words, along with something troubling—a visible tension in his face.

"You girls stay here and set the table while I talk to Daddy," Babi said to Bethie and Vivian. She left the kitchen and went into the living room. Danny started to innocently follow her, but Bethie held him back. Something had happened. For all I knew, someone in the family had already been eaten by the leopard.

Bethie and Vivian took down plates and bowls from the kitchen cabinets, glancing worryingly at each other from time to time as they set the table in the breakfast room. They could hear, and I could hear, my grandparents' voices as they whispered to each other in the living room. I couldn't make out what they were saying, but I didn't like Big Dan's stern, flat tone, or something wounded and challenging in Babi's responses. The thought of my grandparents in conflict felt as disorienting as the drunken men with guns cruising down the street outside our house honking their horns.

While they were talking, I heard Frank's car in the driveway as it pulled past the house to the garage below the apartment he shared with Emmett. Because the two of them worked downtown only a few blocks apart—Frank at Big Dan's Chevrolet dealership and Emmett at Miss Esmerelda's Home for Disappointed Artists—they drove there and back together most days, and usually the first thing they both did was come into the main house for dinner.

But this time, after we heard the angry slam of a car door, it was only Emmett who came into the house, not his brother. He walked through the kitchen and into the breakfast room, where all of us except Big Dan and Babi were. Emmett looked agitated.

"What's wrong?" Bethie said.

"You talked to Dad?"

"No, he's in the living room with Mother."

He started to speak, but when he noticed Danny and me, he did his best to change the subject and brighten his tone of voice. "Hey, did I smell noodle soup?"

"Why don't you boys go upstairs for a minute?" Bethie told us.

"Why?" Danny said.

"Because there are some grown-up things we need to talk about before dinner."

"What things?"

"Grown-up things, I said."

"Why can't we—"

"Scoot!"

She said the word with such explosive force that we knew enough not to argue with her. We ran to the carpeted stairway between the kitchen and the living room, and up to the second floor. Had we been up there by ourselves when the mood in the house was normal, we would have done what we usually did— explore the depths of our grandparents' closet, which was rich with the smell of mothballs and whose floor was crowded with Babi's shoeboxes. Once or twice we had found not-yet-wrapped Christmas presents in there, or the toy promo cars that Big Dan had brought home from the dealership and not yet given to us. The closet was always worth exploring, no matter how many times we had already done so. It was a magic space in which things could spontaneously appear.

But we were too distracted by what was happening downstairs to give the closet much thought at the moment. Danny signaled to me to be quiet and we stealthily made our way to the landing halfway down the stairs. By now our grandparents had left the living room and rejoined the rest of the family in the breakfast room, where everyone seemed to be speaking at once, interjecting and arguing and urging one another to keep their voices down so the children wouldn't be upset.

I couldn't make much of it out—just words and phrases that erupted out of the general chatter with horrifying inscrutability. Big Dan had "fired" our uncle Frank. I had never heard that word used as a verb—"fired." The only conclusion my five-year-old mind could reach was that our grandfather had set our uncle on fire. Why? Was he dead? Would we never see him again?

It was too shocking and interior a thought for me to share

with Danny, so I said nothing as the adult conversation down-stairs continued, growing less understandable all the time. After a while there was silence, and we heard footsteps coming through the kitchen toward the stairwell, so we raced back to our grandparents' room. We heard Emmett climbing the stairs two at a time. "All right, you two," he called out, "your mother says it's time for you to come downstairs for dinner."

He reached down to pick us up off the floor and carry us downstairs. He lacked his brother's natural strength and ath-letic ability, so he didn't scoop us up as fluidly as Frank usually did, but the playful uncle gesture was familiar and, at least to some degree, reassuring. But that sense of all being right with the world was only momentary. It vanished when we sat down to dinner and Big Dan made the sign of the cross and said grace, and I saw that the place where Frank usually sat was empty—evidence that his "firing" had indeed happened and that he was dead.

I stared down at my plate, with the shallow bowl on top of it that contained the dinner I was expected to eat. Noodle soup was my favorite of Babi's Czech-inspired meals, and there was something about even her tableware that I had always found calming. The dishes had decorations of pink flowers and green leaves and brown stems, rendered in such pale colors, such restrained brushwork, that I sensed a puzzling purpose on the part of their creators to stop short of the full visual reality of the things that were being represented. This was tantalizing to me, as was the fact that the flowers and leaves were raised slightly above the surface of the plates, inviting me to trace my fingers along them and to satisfy a child's incessant tactile craving. I inherited a few cracked pieces of my grandmother's Franciscan Desert Rose place settings—just mementoes these days, never used—and when I look at them now I remember the comforting sense of familiarity that came with sitting down together most nights of the week at a table crowded with grown-ups who seemed to Danny and me to exist for no purpose other than to keep us happy and safe.

But that feeling of comfort was glaringly absent tonight. Big Dan sat at one end of the table, Babi at the other. There was an invisible turbulence between them, like the gap between the opposing poles of our toy magnets.

And nobody was talking. The last words that had been said were "In the name of the Father, the Son, and the Holy Ghost," when Big Dan had made the concluding sign of the cross after he said grace.

"This is ridiculous," my mother finally said. "I'm going to go over there and tell him to come to dinner, at least."

"He won't come," Emmett said. "Let him alone."

"Listen now," Big Dan said, with some bite in his voice. "I had to do it. The way he was speaking to Jerome today in front of everybody."

Babi took a sip of soup without looking at him, then said in a tone of contained hostility I had never heard her use with anybody, "He's your son."

"I'm running a dealership, Bernice. I'm running a business. I have to have the trust of my employees, and if they think being fired is something that can never happen to—"

"Did Frank burn up?"

That was me speaking. I remember saying those words in a trembling and confused voice. I remember the image in my head—my uncle Frank standing alone in a sea of fire on the sales floor of Chickasaw Chevrolet. And I remember the looks of the adults who stared at me in astonishment for the suspended moment it took for them to realize the origin of my misunderstanding. Then all the tension seemed to disappear and they began to smile and laugh, though softly and lovingly, careful to make sure I wasn't crushed with embarrassment.

So "fired" was just a word. It didn't have anything to do with being set on fire, my mother told me. There is nothing wrong, she said, nothing for you boys to worry about, Frank was just a little bit upset about something that had happened at work, eat your soup so we can go back to the apartment and get ready for bed.

Dinner was over and Bethie and Vivian were clearing the dishes when Frank walked in through the back door. He was holding a rifle, a big rifle with a heavy wooden stock and a canvas sling. Everyone stared at him with alarm for a moment, and I didn't know whether to be scared or not.

"Now look here," Big Dan said. "What are you doing with that?"

"I just finished cleaning it," Frank told him. He was looking straight into his father's eyes. "I thought we might need it."

"Why would we need a rifle?"

"Because there's a leopard on the loose. And because I don't want Bethie and the boys walking back to the house without somebody to protect them. That suit you all right, Dad?"

"You been drinking?"

"Yes, I did indeed drink one beer, and after I make sure that Bethie and the boys are home safe I may drink another."

It took a moment for everyone to gauge whether he was telling the truth. Bethie must have been the first to decide that he was, because she turned to us and said, "Okay, boys, it's time to go home."

It was only about a hundred feet from the back door of

the main house to the door leading to our apartment and the garage unit above where Frank and Emmett lived, but it seemed to me that night to be a long and dangerous distance. The adults were overreacting. There were about a quarter of a million people living in Oklahoma City at that time, in a metropolitan area of roughly sixty-five square miles. The chances against any of us being attacked by a perplexed animal that had escaped from a zoo six miles away were astronomical. But Danny and I knew nothing about odds, and the three grownups who served as our escort that night had all witnessed death spring at them from unexpected and unlikely directions. I was frightened enough not to object when Emmett picked me up. Danny refused to be carried and tried to refuse even to hold Bethie's hand, relishing the thrill of walking across the exposed concrete. But Bethie wouldn't let him out of her grip, and the more he pulled the tighter her grip became.

"You're hurting me!" he said.

"I don't care! You're holding my hand."

While Emmett held me in his arms, I scanned the territory all around us: the small patch of yard between the main house and the apartment on my left, the row of trees on my right that bordered the neighbors' driveway, the gate ahead with the metal dogs that led through the hedge to the dark expanse of the park. It seemed strange to me that I could still hear the sound of tennis balls from the court in the park. Didn't those people know that the leopard could spring out at them at any moment?

Our little expedition made its way silently across those hundred feet of concrete. Holding me, Emmett was turned with his back exposed to the night, so that if the leopard pounced it would grab him and not the child in his arms. Frank walked with his rifle on the other side, the two adult brothers naturally arranging themselves into defensive flanks to protect their sister and her two sons. In the glow from my grandparents' porch light, I could see the expressions on their faces. For all the tension in the household tonight, my uncles in this moment looked resolute. This chance opportunity to be useful, to settle our fears and guard against the night, seemed to calm and satisfy them.

9

The sound of a helicopter flying low above our house abruptly woke me the next morning. Danny heard it too. We ran from our bedroom in our pajamas to look out the picture window and see the high-domed aircraft with the Army insignia on its side thrumming through our neighborhood skies.

"Morning, sleepyheads," Bethie said as she walked into the living room with an armload of laundry. She was already dressed, though not for work. It was her day off. Though it always made me feel proud in some way I couldn't quite understand to see her in her nurse's uniform, with her white cap and white pinafore apron with "St. Anthony's Hospital" stitched into it in red thread, the sight of that outfit also carried an undercurrent of worry, since it meant she would soon be off to someplace where we weren't allowed to follow. But she wasn't wearing the uniform this morning and there was no threat of her absence—she would be home with us all day.

As I look back, it seems odd that I could have made it all

the way through to the morning without being seized by night-mares; but somehow the escaped leopard didn't intrude upon my dreams and I was in a bright, secure childhood mood that morning as I sat at our little breakfast table with Bethie and Danny. Even with all the close relatives that surrounded us and guarded us, I knew that it was the three of us who made up the irreducible family core. It was not just that we lived apart from the others in our own little household, separated from the main house by a concrete driveway and by our uncles in the garage apartment overhead by a stairway. It was the sense that my identity did not really exist beyond my mother's and brother's, that nature and circumstance had compressed the three of us into a nuclear tightness.

While we were eating our Sugar Corn Pops we heard our uncles' busy footsteps going up and down the stairway on the other side of the kitchen.

"What are Frank and Emmett doing?"

"Nothing. Eat your cereal."

She was in the living room. We heard the familiar screech that the legs of the ironing board made as she pulled them down, and we used the noise to pretend we hadn't heard her. We abandoned our breakfast and ran past her to investigate, but she intercepted us before we could reach the screen door that led from the staircase into the driveway.

"Don't you boys dare go outside! Don't you remember there's a leopard loose?"

"But what are they doing?" Danny said.

"You two stay here."

Bethie walked outside to confront her brothers. From behind the screen door, we could see Frank and Emmett conferring over a map spread out on the hood of Frank's car. Frank held his rifle in his left arm as he and Emmett compared some point on the map with another map that had been printed that morning in *The Daily Oklahoman*.

"Oh, really, this is so childish," Bethie told them.

Neither of them even bothered to respond at first, though Emmett looked up at his sister and sort of smiled.

"I thought at least *you* would have more sense than this, Emmett," she said.

"Come on, Bethie, there's no harm in us having a little fun."

That was the word he used: "fun." But I sensed even then it was a weak word to describe something unfamiliar in Emmett's manner—a surge of real animation and purpose.

Frank gestured toward Bethie with the newspaper. "It says here there are already three thousand people out there hunting the leopard, so why not us?"

He turned back to consult with Emmett. "And you can be sure that most of them are just going to be hanging out around the zoo, but if I were that leopard I'd be long gone, I'd be—" he pointed to the map—"maybe here, way up here around Deep Fork."

Bethie gave up with an annoyed shrug, came back into the house, and shooed us back to the breakfast table.

"Your uncle Frank thinks he knows what that leopard's thinking," she said.

"Does he?" I asked.

"Of course he doesn't. I was being sarcastic."

She went back to her ironing.

"Are they going to shoot the leopard?" I asked.

"They're going to try," Bethie said, with an impatient edge to her voice. "But you two are going to sit here at this table and eat your breakfast. And you know what?"

"What?"

"Later today, if you're good—"

She broke off the sentence and turned her head toward the door again. We could hear Big Dan's voice in the driveway.

"What do the two of you think you're doing?"

Before our mother could stop us Danny and I ran to the screen door again. We saw Big Dan standing a few yards away from his sons as they made their preparations for their leopard safari.

"Don't you suppose you're a little old for this leopard nonsense?"

"Not if we're the ones to shoot it," Frank said.

I didn't like the disapproving look on my grandfather's face as he stood there watching his sons folding up their map and their newspaper and setting their rifles in the back seat of the car. I didn't like the way they refused to meet his eyes—Frank taking obvious pleasure in doing so, Emmett with an edge of discomfort.

"Those rifles loaded?" Big Dan said. It was a question, but it sounded more like an accusation.

Frank nodded dismissively, still avoiding his father's eyes.

"Pretty dangerous out there, if you ask me," he went on, "more dangerous than any escaped leopard. Everybody joyriding around with loaded guns, without the first idea of how to—"

Frank had had enough lecturing. He opened the car door, grabbed the rifle he had just put in the back seat, and took it out and held it up in front of Big Dan's face.

"You know what this is, Dad? It's the same M1 I carried all the way through Europe. Want me to fieldstrip it for you, put it back together? Fine—give me about twenty seconds! Anything you want to teach me about how to handle it? I'm all ears. Emmett is too, aren't you, Emmett? And we'd sure be grateful for your expert advice about hunting leopards, since we've never hunted anything that didn't shoot back."

"Drop that tone right now, Frank. I know you boys went through some things over there that—"

"No, Dad, that's something you don't know anything about, so don't pretend you do."

He had already thrown the rifle back into the back seat, slipped in behind the wheel, and slammed the door. With a glance toward Big Dan that I couldn't process—maybe a look of apologetic complicity or of mutual defiance—Emmett got in as well, and the car lurched backward out of the driveway and onto the street in front of the house.

Big Dan watched them go and then just kept standing there.

"Breakfast!" Bethie said, sweeping past us and closing the screen door behind her. "Now! I'm not going to tell you again."

But we lingered there anyway, boldly ignoring her, watching her as she talked to our grandfather on the driveway. We understood she was trying to calm him down, but he wasn't looking at her, he was still staring off toward the street, his face flushed with anger.

We spent the rest of the morning in the main house. The newspaper had reported that leopards hunted mostly at night, but Big Dan still made a point of escorting Bethie and Danny and me over from our apartment. Vivian was at work, and Danny and I were allowed to watch TV while Bethie and our grandparents drank coffee and had a whispered conversation in the breakfast room with the newspaper—with its multiple stories and illustrations about the escaped leopard—spread out on the table before them. *Sky King* had just started when the show was abruptly interrupted. On the screen now was a newscaster interviewing the same man, the big-cat hunter, we had seen earlier. He was now wearing a safari jacket and talking about a leopard in India that once had killed 125 people.

"They're born killers," he said. "They're mean animals. You back them into a corner and they'll definitely take you on. I would advise all the people out there looking for the leopard today to go home and leave this hunt to the professionals."

"Boys," Bethie announced when she appeared in front of us and switched off the television. We waited to hear what she would say next as the screen gathered itself into a vanishing blip of light and then went dark. The way televisions turned off in those days was like the creation of the universe in reverse.

"Get ready. We're going to the movies right after lunch. Hugh is going to take us all to see *Son of Paleface*."

"Why is Hugh taking us?" I asked. It was a natural question, if not exactly an innocent one. I think I must have been aware of something not quite authentic in her voice, an effort to sound spontaneous about an outing that had been painstakingly concocted.

"Because he wants to get to know us better, especially you two. And because he likes movies, just like you do. Roy Rogers is in it. I know you boys like Roy Rogers."

We did like Roy Rogers, but it was strange how warily we

ate our fried baloney sandwiches for lunch and waited for the mysterious Hugh to come pick us up. We could sense Bethie's nervousness, along with the hovering anticipation of our grandparents. Once again, I had the impression he was the source of some slow-moving but monumental change, a development that everybody was prepared for but me.

If we needed evidence that Hugh was a stranger, it soon came when he rang the front doorbell. Our family exclusively came and went through the back door off the kitchen. When Big Dan set down his newspaper and opened the front door, it felt like something elaborate and rehearsed. Once more I watched my grandfather shake hands with Hugh, a formal gesture I had never seen him make with his own sons.

Hugh wore a sport shirt, pleated pants, and brown shoes that looked new. He stood there comfortably in those shoes, exchanging pleasantries with Big Dan and Babi. They talked about the leopard, the crazy hunters still out on the streets with their rifles and packs of dogs, the breathless coverage of it in the newspaper.

"I don't suppose you young men are afraid of a leopard," he said to Danny and me when he spotted us watching from a distance, near the foot of the stairs at the back of the living room. Before we could think of anything to answer, Bethie came down the stairs. She had changed clothes upstairs in Vivian's room—no doubt she had consulted her sister about what to wear and had likely borrowed one of her dresses. A purse, smaller and a different color from the one she usually carried, hung from her elbow. There was something charged and tentative about the way she and Hugh greeted each other. Maybe shaking hands would have seemed too strained, a kiss on the cheek too presumptuous. So they just stood there a few feet apart and smiled awkwardly in the presence of Danny and me and our grandparents.

Hugh drove us to the Will Rogers Theatre in a commodious blue Oldsmobile 88. He drove with his left hand on the wheel and his right arm stretched across the top of the front seat, his hand almost but not quite touching the back of our mother's neck. Every now and then he would glance toward the back seat, where Danny and I sat, attempting to engage us in a conversation that resulted in only yes-or-no answers from us. He had never been married. He had spent much of his youth as a roustabout in South American oil fields and was now a landman in Texas. He was unaccustomed to children and he must have been as nervous that day as we were perplexed.

"Look at that," he said at one point, as several military trucks with canvas tops passed us on Western Avenue. Inside them, we could see, were men in uniform with rifles. "They've called out the Marines. They must be headed out to the northeast part of the city. That's where the newspaper says the leopard probably is."

"I don't care where he is, as long he's not around my children," Bethie said.

"There were jaguars in the Argentine," Hugh said. He turned to us again. "They're sort of like leopards."

"Did you ever see one?" Danny asked, the first time either of us had been bold enough to speak to him directly.

"No, but I saw plenty of wildlife. Once we were swimming across a river and the local people kept screaming at us from the bank. They were yelling, "Yacare! Yacare!" We didn't know what "yacare" meant until we reached the other side and looked back at the river. Guess what we saw in the water?"

"What?"

"Alligators. Lots of them."

"Alligators eat people," my brother confirmed.

"That's right, Danny, they do."

"Why don't we stop talking about animals eating people," Bethie said. Her tone sounded lighthearted, but I hadn't forgotten the panic in her face the day before, or the fact that the leopard that had leapt up at Danny and me on that visit to the zoo was still at large somewhere in Oklahoma City.

Son of Paleface was a comedy western with Bob Hope and, as Bethie promised, Roy Rogers. Hope played a dandy from Harvard who had come west to claim his inheritance from his father, a supposedly famous Indian fighter. Jane Russell was an improbable stagecoach robber and saloon chanteuse. None of this detail registered with me at the time—I've learned it by watching the movie again online. At the age I was then, even the simplest movie was a raging river of information that swept before me too fast and relentlessly to be understood. But there was nothing frustrating about that. I could accept the sliver of the story I was able to grasp without the anxiety that adults have of missing something crucial. It was a shock, though, to see Roy Rogers in color and projected onto the screen a thousand times larger than he appeared on our tiny black-and-white television. The state-of-the-art Technicolor made his costume violently real. I knew Roy Rogers was a cowboy, so it made sense to me that he would be wearing a western shirt with an elaborate white fringe across the chest, but Bob Hope's Harvard beanie and crimson-and-white-striped jacket were as odd as his character's motivations. It didn't matter—he was funny. He drank a big stein of something potent at a saloon bar and it made smoke come out of his ears and set his body and his head spinning in opposite directions. Danny and I were thrilled by these primitive movie effects. I laughed so hard I could feel my stomach cramping. But when I became aware that my mother and Hugh were watching me, smiling at each other in the darkness of the movie theater, bound together by my reaction to Bob Hope's pratfalls, I grew self-conscious and resentful. It was one thing for my mother to gaze down at me in my seat, her face relaxed and aglow with happiness at the good time her sons were having. It was another thing to know that Hugh was watching as well, and that my hysterical laughing was somehow making me vulnerable, giving him an opening into our tight three-person family he might not otherwise have had.

Maybe that was why, on the drive home, I refused to speak.

"Don't you think you boys should thank Hugh for taking us to the show?" Bethie said to us from the front seat.

"Thank you," Danny said.

"Grady?" my mother said.

"What?"

"Are you going to say thank you to Hugh?"

But I kept my mouth shut and stared defiantly out the window. A convertible drove by filled with young men brandishing shotguns, cruising the streets looking for the leopard. They were only teenagers, but to me they looked old and threateningly virile.

"Honey?"

"Oh, don't worry about it," Hugh told her. "He doesn't have to say anything."

"Well, he certainly should," Bethie said. She punished me by turning her face from me and staring pointedly out the windshield at the road ahead.

When we got home that afternoon, Hugh came along with us into our grandparents' house, settling comfortably into one of the living-room chairs and talking with Big Dan about cars and baseball and how the highways in Texas, where he lived, were better than those in Oklahoma.

"I sure had fun today with your grandsons," he said. He was looking over at us now, smiling, a little formal, a little uncertain. I still stubbornly kept myself from looking back in his direction. It's easy enough now to put myself into Hugh's situation that afternoon—a man falling in love with someone, wanting to win over her children, finding it to be a harder task than he had imagined, especially with the younger boy, who for some reason or another refused to look in his direction.

He had done nothing wrong. He had been careful and kind. It wasn't his fault that I regarded his presence as a threat to a universe that I imagined had already been specifically constructed for me. After the last few days, I was beginning to sense how unstable that universe was, how it could all be broken apart through some unexpected vector, by some outside force. I couldn't tolerate the way my mother seemed not to know that. I didn't like the unfamiliar glimmer of happiness I detected in her eyes whenever she looked at Hugh, a lightness of spirit that should have only been for us.

Mixed in with those hazy emotions was a clear awareness of my own childhood cruelty. I knew what I was doing in not answering Hugh, in not meeting his eyes, in not expressing any gratitude for taking us to see *Son of Paleface*. It must have been that realization, as much as anything, that made me explode into tears and race up the stairs to my grandparents' room and hide under their bed.

Lying there, I could hear Danny downstairs loudly asking, "What's wrong with him?" and Bethie answering him that I was just a little upset about something and to leave me alone. I could hear the voices of my grandparents speaking in a hushed, apologetic tone as they talked to Hugh, and I could hear my mother speaking to him in a softer voice in words I couldn't make out. Then I heard her footsteps on the carpeted stairs, and after a moment I saw her face. She was on her knees, bending down, looking at me from beneath the bed frame, smiling sadly.

"Honey," she said, "won't you come out of there? I'd like to talk to you."

I shook my head.

"Well, do you think there's room for me under the bed with you?"

"I don't know."

"I can try. Is that okay?"

My grandparents' bed was an old-fashioned four-poster that sat high enough off the floor for Bethie to squeeze herself beneath it and scooch over to where I lay cowering. She put her arms around me and stroked my hair. I had stopped crying by then, though I was determined to remain angry for as long as I could. But it was hard to be angry when I had my mother all to myself in a secret hiding place. The dormer windows of my grandparents' bedroom were open, and when I looked out through the bottom of the bed I could see the summer-afternoon light, filtered through the swaying curtains, moving and retreating like a tide across the deep carpet, lazily illuminating the amoeba-like patterns imprinted there. I remember the smell of the freshly laundered sheets on the bed above me, and the silky feel of the blue summer dress my mother wore as she hugged me against her shoulder.

For a long time Bethie didn't say anything. Then she finally asked, in a very soft voice, what was wrong.

"I'm afraid of the leopard," I told her.

Was that the reason? Maybe not quite, not in that moment anyway, but I didn't know what else to say to account for my behavior. I was scared of the leopard, true enough, but there was something else on the loose that I had no name for and no capacity to identify. I didn't like the way people were acting. It was not just the crazy hunters out on the streets who were filled with perplexing excitement, but my family as well. My mother was panicky and protective, but at the same time I could sense some reckless undercurrent when she was around Hugh, a strange new interest that extended perilously beyond the bounds of what I understood about her and where her primary attention belonged. I might even have felt, absurd as it sounds when she was hugging me tight beneath my grandparents' bed, that I was about to be abandoned.

"You know what?" she whispered. "I think you're a lot like me."

"I am?"

"Yes. Maybe you feel things a little too much. But you know something else?"

"What?"

"You're a little bit like your father too, but you just don't know it yet."

There under the bed she talked to me for the first time about the father I had never known. How he had had no fear of anything, how his sense of fun and adventure had swept her up from the first time she met him, during the war when she was an Army nurse and he was a fighter pilot who had been shipped home from the Pacific and ended up in the base hospital with malaria. The more she described him, the way he looked, the joy he took in flying and taking risks, the way his thoughts were always trained on the goal he had in mind and were never bothered by scenarios of what could go wrong—the more I thought of Danny climbing up to the next tier of that memorial fountain, and his frustration and bewilderment that I was too scared to follow him. I didn't really believe that what Bethie said was true—it was Danny who was like our father, not me—but I wanted it to be true. I wanted to think of myself as someone more than the cowering little brother whose imagination was constantly inflamed with danger and foreboding.

She said nothing more, just lingered with me for a while in a long, soothing silence before asking if I was ready to come out.

"Not yet."

"Well, you just stay here for as long as you want to, then."

She kissed me on my forehead, then slid out from beneath the bed, ruffling the fringes of the bedspread as she went.

10

I stayed beneath the bed for probably another half hour, staring up at the box spring, listening to the residential traffic on the street outside the open window. I felt happily depleted. Whatever point my five-year-old mind had tried to make, it seemed to have made.

It was late afternoon by then, but still bright summer daylight outside. I could hear Big Dan and Hugh talking easily downstairs as they watched a ball game on TV. Danny was still with them, asking questions about the teams or the players with a confidence that left me feeling even more isolated. At the age we were then, a year's difference represented to me a whole lifetime of advanced knowledge and experience. In the upstairs bedroom, I was too far away to make out anything specific that was being said, and televised baseball was still such a mystery to me it wouldn't have made much difference. But the rhythm of the conversation was clear enough, the easy give-and-take when Danny asked a question and Big Dan patiently answered. It unsettled me to hear Hugh joining the conversation, speaking as familiarly to my brother as if he were now a member of the family.

"What were you doing?" Danny demanded to know when I finally slipped out from under the bed and walked down the stairs. He was sprawled out in one of our grandparents' matching green corduroy armchairs. Big Dan sat in the other armchair, and Hugh sat upright in one of the hardback chairs from the bridge table on the other side of the room.

"Nothing," I told Danny. Big Dan reached out his arm and drew me over to him. "There he is," he said, as he pulled me onto his lap. "Watch this, Grady. Hank Sauer's up."

"Mr. Quicksand himself," Hugh said. He and Big Dan chuckled knowingly at this shared reference. Hugh leaned forward in his chair, looking at Danny and then at me. "That's what they called the Cubs outfield," he said. "The Quicksand Kids. They weren't exactly known for being fast."

"Is there really such a thing as quicksand?" Danny asked him, as casually as if he were asking a question of Big Dan or one of our uncles, as if Hugh had already established himself as a member of our family without anybody questioning why.

"Oh, sure," he said. "I was trying to buy a lease once from an old rancher down around the Pecos River. He said they lose cattle to quicksand all the time."

"Does it swallow up people?" I was surprised to hear myself ask this question, since until then I had spoken to Hugh only grudgingly, when Bethie insisted I do so. But it was an urgent issue, since I had long been plagued by a blood-freezing memory from a *Jungle Jim* movie or an episode of *Ramar of the Jungle:* a man being sucked down inch by inch, slowly buried alive in a viscous black grave, until only his mud-caked hand was left, reaching out forlornly for help.

Hugh turned to me with a grateful, relaxed look in his eyes, the look of someone who thought he might be breaking through at last.

"Oh, I don't think so, Grady," he said. "That's just in the movies probably. I don't think you have to worry about that at all."

I was relieved to hear this news, but I didn't want him to think that the tension between us was broken, so when Big Dan called out "It's a homer!" I abruptly shifted my eyes away from Hugh and toward the All-Star game on the television screen, where in soft-focus black-and-white Hank Sauer was running the bases in his billowy uniform.

"I wonder why they haven't put Mantle in," Big Dan said to Hugh. "He's from Oklahoma, you know?"

"Oh, yes, from somewhere up there in Cherokee country, I think."

"His father's name is Mutt. I bet old Mutt Mantle is proud of his son."

On the television, the base runner had not yet made it home when the game was interrupted by another bulletin. The announcer was alerting the citizenry that fresh leopard tracks had been discovered near an old stone bridge several miles from the zoo. He held up a crude map to show the location, then turned to the bullet-headed expert.

"What do these footprints tell us?" the announcer asked him.

"Very little," he replied. "He was at this bridge today. Tomorrow he could be anywhere. The man-eater of Rudraprayag, for instance, had a killing range of five hundred square miles."

No one turned the television off at that point. My mother and Babi were in the kitchen, where they had probably retreated in order to give Big Dan and Hugh a chance to get to know each other over a baseball game. They must have been deep enough in conversation to have not yet heard or noticed that the ball game was no longer on and the on-screen conversation had switched to man-eating leopards. Vivian was out somewhere, Hugh probably didn't consider it his place to suggest turning off the TV or changing the channel in someone else's home, and Big Dan must have been too riveted by the leopard story, too concerned about his troubled sons who were out there right now prowling around with guns like the rest of Oklahoma City, to think to worry about the overactive imaginations of the five- and six-year-old boys in the room with him.

In any case, we heard all about the famous man-eating leopard of Rudraprayag, who a half century before had killed 125 people along the pilgrim roads of northern India. Not just killed them, but silently opened the latches of the doors to their huts, or clawed through the mud walls, and in the middle of the night seized children from beside their sleeping mothers and carried them off into the darkness.

"This terrible leopard," the television expert said, "had developed such a taste for human flesh that no one was safe. Not women, not children, not strong adult men. A husband might be sitting together with his wife, eating his dinner, and suddenly feel the last thing he would ever feel—the fangs of the creature biting through his neck."

"Well, that's nonsense," Big Dan said in response to this overdramatic commentary, as he remembered that Danny and

I were in the room. He got up from his chair and walked over and switched off the television. "I'm not a big-game hunter, but I'll bet you any amount of money that that poor leopard is scared out of his mind right now."

He turned to us. "No reason for you boys to be afraid."

But we *were* afraid, or at least I was. In fact, I had just entered a new register of fear. Up until then I had felt vulnerable only when out in the open, as we made our way down the driveway from the safety of my grandparents' house to the sanctuary of our apartment. Now, according to this expert on television, I was no longer safe behind closed doors. The leopard had the ability to infiltrate locked doors and windows, to stand there with exquisite silence and stillness in our living room as it decided which one of us to carry away—me or Danny or my mother.

"Hugh," said Babi, who had just now appeared in the living room along with Bethie. She was wearing an apron and holding a wooden spoon. "Won't you stay for dinner?"

"Thank you, Mrs. Brennan, but—"

"Oh, please, it's Bernice."

"Bernice. It's very kind of you to ask, but maybe some other time. I'm going to take my mother out to dinner before I head back to Midland in a few days."

"Oh? Midland? Well, I hope we'll see you again soon."

He said, with a glance at my mother that did not escape my scrutiny, that he would probably see everybody again before he left, and in any case would be back in Oklahoma City again in a few weeks. He was on the verge of taking his leave when we heard the back door open.

"It's the boys," Bethie said. She meant the other "boys"— not Danny and me, her sons, but Frank and Emmett, the two brothers for whom she had long ago, as their sister, assigned to herself a parental responsibility. She hurriedly slipped away to head them off in the kitchen. She must have known they had been drinking and didn't want them to interfere with the carefully choreographed goodbye tableau with Hugh that was taking place in the other part of the house. But if that was her intention, she didn't succeed. We heard a few fragments of worried conversation, and then my uncles appeared in the living room, their shoes and pant cuffs muddy, their faces sunburnt.

"The fearless leopard hunters are home!" Frank announced. He leaned against the doorjamb, his hands in his pockets, surveying the room with a conniving grin. "Hello, Dad," he said.

Big Dan responded to his son's greeting with a curt nod.

Frank shrugged, as if he had expected Big Dan's disapproval and welcomed it. Then he noticed Hugh, who had been standing by the front door about to make his exit when my uncles arrived. "Hello there again," Frank said. He crossed the room to shake Hugh's hand. He gripped it a little too tightly. Frank's eyes were bright, he was smiling at Hugh, but there was something unfriendly and challenging about the smile that made me nervous. He was drunk in a different way than he had been when he was out on the driveway making us look up in the sky at the comet. He had been sloppy that night, but today he was composed and focused in a way that made him seem even more foreign.

"You know what, Hugh?" Frank said. "You should come out leopard hunting with us tomorrow."

"Well, thanks for the invitation, Frank, but it looks like you and Emmett are going to have to kill the leopard yourselves. I've got some work to do before I head back to Texas."

"Aw, work can wait. Don't you want to be part of the biggest thing that's ever happened in Oklahoma City?"

Hugh responded with a companionable chuckle, but Frank wouldn't let it go at that.

"Come on," he said. "You've got a rifle, don't you?"

"Not with me."

"Well, you can buy one, then. You know that big sporting-goods store on Grand? They had a sign in the window today—what did it say exactly, Emmett?"

"'Headquarters for All Your Leopard-Hunting Needs,'" Emmett said. He had taken a seat and was monitoring his older brother's interrogation of Hugh. I couldn't read his expression. He might have been alarmed, he might have been amused, he might have just been wearily drunk.

"You boys should come along too," Frank said, pivoting away from Hugh and toward Danny and me. "Might not get another chance. There are kids almost your age all over the place, carrying their twenty-twos. Might be the last chance you ever have to go leopard hunting."

"My children are not going leopard hunting." Bethie's voice was lethally calm.

"I bet Burt would have let them," Frank said. As soon as he said it, drunk as he was, he must have known he had wandered across an invisible barrier. Our dead father was spoken of so rarely in that house that the mere mention of his name was something that made everyone warily attentive. And now Frank seemed to be deploying that name as a way of rebuking his sister for some offense I was unequipped to imagine.

There was a hovering moment of silence in the room; then Emmett said, "Take it easy, Frank."

"Take *what* easy?" He turned once again to Hugh. "Do *you* know what I'm not taking easy?"

"Frank," Babi said. "You and Emmett go out to the apartment and get cleaned up. Then we'll have dinner."

"Yeah, Mom's right," Emmett said. "Let's go."

"Yeah, okay, just a minute. I just want to ask Hugh here something first."

"All right, Frank," Hugh said.

"Just wanted to know if you're planning to marry Bethie."

"That's enough, Frank," Big Dan said.

"It's just a question, Dad. What's wrong with me asking a question?"

"For Christ's sake," Emmett said.

"Are you planning to marry my sister?" Frank said to Hugh. "Are you planning to raise these boys?"

"I think your mother's right, Frank," Hugh replied, with a friendly pat on Frank's shoulder, "Maybe you should get sobered up and—"

Frank swatted away Hugh's hand, and he didn't stop there. He gave him a shove. It wasn't a shove, really, just a gesture—a slight push of the palm of his hand against Hugh's chest. But even I could recognize it as a clear, if inebriated, display of dominance.

"Oh," Frank said, still smiling. "Thank you for informing me how I need to behave in my own house."

I could see the anger flaring in Hugh's eyes as he took a step backward from Frank's shove, and I saw it disappear in an instant. He had no intention of getting into a fight with Bethie's brother, not in front of her and not in front of her children. He didn't put up his hands, either in defense or in aggression, but he didn't look away, either. He held Frank's eyes and said nothing. I could see, after a moment, that Frank was shamed, diminished by Hugh's sober self-possession.

"Aw, hell," Frank said. "You didn't do anything."

Hugh said not to worry about it, and that he had to be leaving. He offered his hand to Frank, who shook it with an embarrassed detachment: then Hugh said goodbye to everyone again. Bethie followed him out the front door, and it was a long time before she came back into the house. By that time Frank and Emmett had retreated to their garage apartment and Big Dan had sat back down in his armchair and picked up the newspaper. He wasn't reading, he was just staring hard at the pages.

"Is everything okay?" Danny asked him. Even Danny had been shaken by what had just taken place.

"Of course everything's okay," Big Dan said. "Go into the kitchen and help your grandmother get dinner ready."

We did as he said, and found Babi standing next to the stove, spooning bacon grease from a coffee can into a cast-iron skillet.

"Big Dan said to come in here," Danny said.

"Oh, he did, did he? Well, come in here, then."

She pivoted away from the stove and the skillet of melting grease and began slicing potatoes on a cutting board. She had also, I noticed, pivoted away from us. She didn't want us to see her crying, but there were tears leaking from below the rims of her cat's-eye glasses. I knew that she was upset, just as Big Dan was, by the altercation that had just taken place in the living room, but at my age I had no way to measure the weight of grief and disappointment bearing down on her.

She set down the knife, grabbed a dish towel, and, lifting her glasses up, dabbed at her eyes.

"Don't worry," she said. "Your uncles love you."

The statement came out of nowhere. I had no idea what she was trying to reassure us about. It hadn't occurred to me that Frank and Emmett might not love us. But we were both too confused by the mysterious tension in the house to ask her to elaborate.

"Are you hungry?" She asked. "Do you want something to eat before dinner?" She started opening cupboards, keeping her tearful face away from us. "I thought I had a can of shoestring potatoes here, but I guess not. Why don't you go into the basement and see if you can find one?"

An invitation to visit the basement on our own, without adult supervision, was unprecedented. But at that moment it must have seemed to Babi a good way to distract us from whatever emotional turmoil we might yet witness if we remained in the aboveground part of the house. The basement was small, just a mildewy chasm where the washing machine was kept, but to us it was a perpetually unexplored continent.

Danny reached up on tiptoe to push the light switch at the top of the stairway just behind the kitchen. We crept down into what seemed like a raw inverse of the surface world: bare light bulbs, uncarpeted wooden stairs, a cement floor laden with things that had been stockpiled or cast off or hidden away. We checked the shelves at the base of the stairs and found no shoestring potatoes, just cans whose labels featured unappetizing images of tomato sauce and pie filling and asparagus. It didn't matter. We weren't nearly as hungry as we were curious about what might be found in a room where cardboard boxes were stacked against three of the walls. There was no telling what sorts of treasure could be found in those boxes. Maybe some intriguing adult artifact, or a toy that one of our relatives had forgotten to give us.

There were a lot of hatboxes and shoeboxes that belonged to Vivian, and they were the right size to hold something more interesting than hats or shoes, but when we lifted the lids we found nothing but tissue paper. We dug out from beneath a pile of other junk a brown military-issue garment bag with a name stamped onto it.

"That's *his* name," Danny said.

"Whose name?"

He showed me the lettering and sounded the words out loud. " 'Captain Burton McClarty.' That's Burt. Our father."

It was a big piece of luggage that folded over on itself and zipped up at the sides. What we found inside when we unzipped it was an Army Air Corps wool uniform jacket, with various medals and insignias pinned or sewn above the breast pocket. There were other things in the suitcase—a pair of Army boots, a paper bag filled with service pins of one sort or another, and a leather-bound photo album with black-and-white snapshots of airplanes sitting on airstrips in jungle clearings, and groups of shirtless men posing in front of them.

"I think that's him," Danny said, pointing to one of the photographs. This one was of a solitary pilot sitting in the cockpit and waving to the photographer. We stared at the familiar-but-unfamiliar face, trying to understand the mystery of how our existence depended upon the vanished man depicted in this photograph. But it was too large a thing for our young minds to ponder for long, so we put the album aside and began sorting through other boxes, boxes full of letters held together in batches with ribbons tied around them, boxes of utility receipts and bank statements and church bulletins, boxes of old shoes and out-of-fashion neckties and varsity letter jackets that had once belonged to our uncles or maybe even to our grandfather.

And there were other photographs, either stuck into albums with old-fashioned photo corners or just lying loose. They had been taken in a time before we were born, most of them in a time before the war. Nostalgia is not an emotion that comes naturally to a five-year-old boy who is senseless to time, for whom the past and the future are abstractions and only the endlessly occurring present is real. But when I looked at these photos of our family as it was before Danny and I were born I felt a strange almost-sadness. Everyone in those photos was younger, of course, but they also looked happier, not at war with each other as they seemed to be now but bound together by an easy understanding of who they were and what their common future would be. There was one picture in particular whose depiction of family serenity made me feel unaccountably agitated. It showed the whole family—our grandparents, our mother, Vivian, Frank, and Emmett—standing on a winter day in front of the house. It must have been taken some time toward the end of the 1930s. Our mother wore a cap and gown—so the occasion had probably been her high-school graduation. Big Dan was in a double-breasted suit, looking younger and slimmer, proudly beaming. Babi wore a white hat with a wide brim and a thick hatband tied in a bow in the front. Vivian and Emmett, both still in high school, were grinning vivaciously. And then there was Frank, also wearing a suit. He had unbuttoned the top button of his shirt and loosened his tie after the graduation ceremony. He had one arm around Bethie and another around his father—a proud big brother and son, already out into the world, already probably working at Chickasaw Chevrolet.

The lightness and ease of the people in that photograph, the obvious comfort they had around one another, forced upon me the unwelcome conclusion that something had gone wrong, that they had once lived in an era of contentment that had vanished before I was born. I knew, with a kind of instinct if not conscious understanding, that this photo had been taken before Frank and Emmett had gone off to war and come back changed, before our mother had become a nurse and witnessed some of the gravest physical casualties of that war, before she had lost her own husband, before the whole family had reestablished itself in the house where they had once been young and whole, but where they were now shadowed by grief, stalled in one way or another from fully moving into the future, and more and more at rancorous cross-purposes.

The world before I entered it, the time that I had always imagined as a gray nothingness, took on a disquieting reality the more I looked at these pictures. There was a time that had been untouched by the war, but everything that followed—maybe even Danny and me—was the result of a world that had been twisted and tainted.

We found pictures of Frank and Emmett and my mother in their Army uniforms, and various typed and mimeographed documents. And there was a Whitman's Sampler candy box that we were disappointed to find wasn't filled with candy but with various odds and ends—military medals and pins, holy cards, a rosary in a zip-up pocket pouch, and more old letters and postcards. None of it was particularly interesting, except for an insignia patch whose bright colors attracted my attention. The patch was diamond-shaped, with a bright-red background rendered in sumptuous three-dimensional thread, and at its center a big, stylized yellow bird, its wings bent at right angles. I didn't know the word "Thunderbird," but I sensed the image had something to do with Indians.

"You can keep it," Danny said when he noticed me running my finger across the stitching.

"I can?"

"Sure, we can keep all this stuff. Nobody cares."

I slipped the patch into the pocket of my short pants and closed the lid to the candy box.

11

In our apartment that night, Bethie let us watch TV before bedtime. This was a rare indulgence. After dinner the order of the evening was always to take our bath, put on our pajamas, and play quietly until it was time for our mother to read to us and put us to bed. But Vivian had been out most of the day and had missed the scene that took place when Frank and Emmett returned from their leopard hunt. She had come over after dinner to hear about it firsthand from her sister.

They talked in near-whispers in Bethie's bedroom while Danny and I sat in front of our television, which was even smaller than the one in the main house, and with poorer reception. There was nothing on at that hour that particularly interested us—no westerns or children's shows—so we had to make do with *My Little Margie,* whose mildly chortling laugh track was our only hint that the show was a comedy. Margie's widowed father looked ancient, with his slicked-back gray hair and pencil mustache. He and his spunky young-adult daughter inhabited a universe of power offices and spacious apartments that, even allowing for the fact that the show was in black-and-white, struck me as suffocatingly colorless. From time to time it was all obscured by a swirl of electronic snow particles, which Danny was able to remedy somewhat by adjusting the rabbit ears on top of the set. Even when the screen image was clear we still had only a faint idea of what was going on between the two main characters. But for children, incomprehension has its own fascination, and we watched the interplay between Margie and her indulgent father without thinking about the conversation taking place between Bethie and Vivian.

When the show was over, Bethie came out of her bedroom, switched the television off, and said, "Okay, to bed. Right now!" We did our usual arguing and stalling, and in the end Bethie conceded that if we got into bed right away Vivian would stay and read us a story. Our aunt sat down in a chair between our beds. It was an undersized children's chair, which made her loom like a giant when we looked up at her from our pillows. She picked up a volume of My Book House, opened it at random, and began to read one of the archaic stories, but she closed the book after only a few lines.

"This is boring," she said. "Don't you have anything more interesting? Let's see if we can find the funny pages."

She set down the book, left the room, and came back a few moments later with the day's newspaper.

"Well," she said, "it's not the Sunday paper but it'll have to do. Let's see what's going on with Mary Worth . . . Uh-oh, more drama. Wilma resents what Edwin calls his 'casual attentions to Mrs. Worth.' What do you boys think? Are his intentions casual? Should we take him at his word? Anyway, Wilma says, 'Edwin! Lover lamb! I'm so relieved to hear you say that!'"

We burst into laughter at the comic emphasis Vivian placed on the words "lover lamb," though we didn't have the faintest idea of what was besetting the people in the comic strip. She moved on to *Terry and the Pirates* and then *Buz Sawyer.* Like *Mary Worth,* they featured adult protagonists with adult problems, rendered in densely inked panels. I was relieved when she turned the page and found *Blondie.* It was lighter and funnier, and for some reason I never tired of contemplating the antenna-like tufts of hair that rose from either side of Dagwood Bumstead's head.

Vivian read the dialogue from the comic strip with theatrical finesse. Her lighthearted rendition of Blondie and Dagwood, and then of *Little Iodine* and *Henry,* was comforting to two boys confused by the tense exchanges that had taken place a few hours earlier in the main house. I had almost forgotten the general terror that was stalking Oklahoma City when I noticed a newspaper photograph of a leopard above the comic strip Vivian was reading from. The photo was of a leopard's face viewed head-on—ears back, fangs bared, eyes focused with vicious precision on its prey. It was impossible to escape the conclusion that its prey was me. When Vivian turned the page and the image disappeared, I could still somehow see it. I could feel it seeping into my consciousness like a permanent stain.

At almost the same moment I heard footsteps on the stairway leading down from the garage apartment upstairs.

"Bethie," Vivian said. Even though she was calling out to our mother in a soft, calm voice, I could tell it was a warning.

"I heard," Bethie called back. She was already on the way to the door. I heard Frank's knock, just before he opened it, and I heard Bethie's angry voice as she intercepted him. "We're getting the boys to bed."

I could tell from the sound of his voice that he was still drunk, but not as drunk as he had been several hours before, and certainly not as belligerent. Vivian closed the door to our bedroom, but we could hear anyway. Frank was telling Bethie that he needed to talk to us, and she was telling him no, that whatever he had to say could wait till morning and to please go back upstairs and go to sleep. Then we heard Emmett's voice as well, at first trying to convince Frank to do what their sister said, and then—after a few more minutes of contentious conversation in hushed voices—saying, "Aw, Bethie, maybe he's right. Do you really think it would do any harm for him just to talk to them?"

There were a few more minutes of negotiations before Bethie finally opened the door to our bedroom and said, in an expressionless voice, "Your uncle Frank would like to talk to you."

Vivian, still seated in the child's chair between our beds, gave Bethie a quizzical glance and then stood up, joining her sister at the open door as Frank entered the room and sat down on the floor.

"Hey, men," he said.

He was quiet for a moment, thinking, and then he started to talk. He talked with a heedless emotional intensity, telling us what fine boys we were, how proud the whole family was of us, how he wanted us to know that.

"You know," he said, "a lot happened in the world before you guys came along. A lot of it was really bad. A lot of it was unfair, like what happened to your mother, being left all alone with two boys with no father. Well, not all alone, because *we* were there, right? All of us. And we all know that the world can't be such a terrible place after all, with the two of you in it."

He went on for a long time in this rambling, maundering way as he sat there on the floor between us. I didn't know if he was really talking to us or talking to himself, because every once in a while he would emphatically nod his head after he finished a sentence, as if he were expressing agreement not with what he had just said but with some unexpressed thought circulating in his mind that only he could access. I didn't dare look up at my mother or Vivian while this was going on, because I knew if I showed my bewilderment I would somehow be betraying Frank. I didn't want to add to their alarm, because it would help verify that something was really wrong, and I didn't want anything to be wrong.

"So I'm sorry, all right? I'm sorry about the way I behaved tonight with Hugh."

"Frank, that's nice," Vivian warned, "but I think—"

"Wait a minute, I just want to tell the boys one other thing about Hugh. Now, I know you two need a father. It's not enough just to have uncles, or I suppose it isn't, and if it turns out that he's—"

"That's enough," Bethie said. Her voice was firm but—for our sakes, I suppose—seemingly friendly and level. "These kids have to go to sleep," she told her brother, "and so do you."

Frank pulled himself to his feet and turned to face Bethie. "Is that an order, Lieutenant Brennan?"

"That's an order, Sergeant Brennan."

Frank gave her a rigid salute that made Danny and me laugh. But Bethie wasn't nearly as amused. "Also, you and Emmett need to walk Vivian home."

"Oh, for Pete's sake," Vivian said. "It's only a hundred feet."

"I don't care. It's almost dark and there's a leopard out there somewhere."

Vivian kissed us good night. I listened as Frank and Emmett walked with her out the front door and made their way toward the main house. It seemed like a long time before my uncles came back and climbed the stairs once again to their garage apartment. I was far from sure they were going to return at all, since the leopard was still out there—and thanks to learning from the television about the man-eating leopard of Rudraprayag, my frightful imaginings had soared.

"We almost forgot to say our prayers," Bethie announced, when everyone had safely returned to their places of residence. She got us out of the covers, and, as we did every night, the three of us knelt at the edge of Danny's bed. We made the sign of the cross and joined our mumbling voices to our mother's as she led us through an Our Father and a Hail Mary and then a less formulaic request to God for the health and safety of all the members of our family.

Then, finally, we all went to bed. Though not to sleep. When Bethie went down the hall to her room, she left Danny and me alone with our raging imaginations.

"Is Bethie going to marry Hugh?" I whispered to my brother across the room.

"I don't know."

"If she did, would he be our father?"

"I guess so. Be quiet."

"Would we have to move to—"

"I said be quiet."

He spoke in a tone of voice that was familiar to me: the chronic annoyance of an older brother. But I knew that it was more than mere impatience. I could sense that, like me, he was struggling to piece together everything that was happening and trying to make sense of it—and that he wanted to think in silence. After I asked a few more nervous, unanswerable questions, he stopped acknowledging them altogether. Then he defiantly fell asleep, or at least I thought he had. He lay in his bed facing the wall, his back toward me, unmoving.

So here I was again in the faint glow of the Hopalong Cassidy night-light, feeling all alone, the only one awake, the only one who would know if the leopard suddenly materialized in the house. But I was also the smallest and weakest and most afraid. The longer I lay there, the more I was convinced I heard the leopard pacing outside the window of our room, the window that faced toward the park. He moved as silently as breath. He knew where we were, and he was patiently searching for a way to slip inside.

Once inside, he could grab me by the throat and bear me away in silence into the awful night without Bethie or Danny or our uncles upstairs in their apartment even knowing about it. But it was even worse to imagine the leopard taking my mother, to think of it grabbing her before she could even scream, and then jumping out the window with her writhing body in its jaws. I tried to picture myself having the courage to chase after the leopard as it bounded through the great park beyond our house, to envision having the speed to overtake it and save my mother, but even to the feverish imagination of a five-year-old boy such a fantasy was out of reach.

As I lay there in growing terror, I thought I could hear the leopard. It was no longer outside but in the house with us, softly growling as it moved from room to room. Any movement I made might alert the beast, so I stayed rigidly still. Just as I had several nights earlier, I desperately wanted to make a dash for Bethie's room and the safety of her bed, but this night was different. Or maybe *I* was different. I had something to call on that I hadn't before, something to do with what my mother had told me as I hid under my grandparents' bed earlier that afternoon. It was the idea that there might be something of my unknown father in me after all, some trace element of daring. During that long night I lay frozen in terror, but also filled with resolve, as I tried to convince myself that what I wanted to believe was true.

12

I finally passed from the torments of wakefulness into a sound sleep, and then woke to a Sunday morning that felt blessedly familiar. Neither Bethie nor Danny nor I had been carried away in the night by the leopard; and maybe because I was so grateful that all of us were still alive, I didn't put up too much of a fight against the weekly requirement to go to Mass in our intolerably itchy church clothes.

I was surprised to see Frank and Emmett waiting for us in the driveway as Bethie hurried us out of the apartment to make sure we got to church on time. They were in their Sunday clothes as well. Although they didn't seem to want to meet our mother's eyes, they greeted us with an insouciance that caught me off guard. I suppose I was expecting the troubles of the day before to be a permanent condition, but now everyone was carrying on as normal—or at least trying to give that impression.

Frank smiled when he saw me at the front door warily scanning my surroundings before I dared to leave the house.

"You know that leopards only attack at night, don't you, Grady? You don't have to worry about them in broad daylight."

"He doesn't care when they attack, and I don't, either," Bethie said. "We're not taking any chances. Hurry up and get in the car."

We climbed in and backed out of the driveway, with our grandparents and Vivian following in Big Dan's car. We drove the few blocks to the church and trooped inside and walked halfway up the aisle. The adults all genuflected and crossed themselves before they entered the pew, one of several sacred protocols that Danny and I were too young to be made to follow. And we were too young to understand anything that was going on in general. All we knew was that every week we had to endure it. The Mass was in Latin back then, though if it had been in English it would not have been any more comprehensible to the two young children trapped in that pew.

I had no idea what sort of secret business was being conducted at the distant altar by a priest with his back turned to the congregation. Above the altar rose the seashell-like vault of the apse, with a bloody Jesus sagging on the cross in agony, and far above him a much more benevolent image of the Virgin Mary holding a baby in her arms. It would be years before I learned that this was the same baby who grew up to be the man nailed to the cross. For now, that serene face looking down upon the people in the church—looking down upon *me*—was uncomplicated and soothing, something to focus on whenever Bethie admonished me to stop squirming.

The ritual was an unending puzzle pageant: everyone standing, then everyone kneeling, then everyone standing and kneeling all over again as the priest raised his arms or lifted the chalice or bowed to the tinkling of the altar boy's bells. It felt to me like the structure we were in—the Cathedral of Our Lady of Perpetual Help—was a great hollow rock in the middle of a river. All around it the waters of time rushed and swirled and went on their way, but to those of us trapped here the flow had stopped. We were hostages to a moment that could never budge.

To try to distract myself from this sonorous eternity, and from the itching of my pants, I fidgeted and moved around to study the gruesome sculptural panels depicting the stations of the cross that lined either wall. They showed Jesus staggering and falling under his cross, a woman wiping his bloody face, Roman soldiers pounding nails into his hands. When I look back on it, all this violent and confusing imagery should have been more of a threat to my mental well-being than the thought of an escaped leopard, but I had swum into consciousness surrounded by so many such renderings that these lurid tableaux of the torturing of Jesus were no more remarkable to me than the sight of the Lone Ranger galloping across the TV screen.

Everyone knelt again, and I dutifully imitated them, though only for the excuse to assume a different position. I felt the plush fabric of the kneeling rail against my bare knees as I set my hands on the hard surface of the pew in front of me. I looked down the length of our own pew, at the faces of my family, all of them except Danny with their hands folded in prayer and their heads bowed. Babi wore a black hat with a stiff, shiny crown, Vivian a red pillbox with a veil whose bottom rim ended just at eye level. My mother's head covering was only a simple scarf that she had tied around her chin as she was walking from the parking lot to the church.

I understood that some sort of harm—spiritual or even physical—would come to women if they didn't cover their heads while they were in church. Men did not have to worry about this, and indeed were supposed to remove their hats when they entered any inside space, but especially the highly charged space of a place of worship. In any case, only Big Dan had come to Mass wearing a hat. It sat beside him on the pew. Frank and Emmett had both dressed up in boxy sport coats and ties, and the resentments that had erupted between them and their father seemed, in this moment, to be suspended. As he knelt, Frank kept his hands clasped and his eyes shut. He muttered along with the Latin phrases that made up the congregation's response to the priest's incantatory pronouncements. The intensity of Frank's prayerful bearing fascinated me. It seemed out of keeping for someone with such a disregard, it not outright contempt, for any sort of compliance. He didn't seem to me like a believer—more like someone who was forcing himself to believe, to fit in with a family that believed.

Maybe everything was all right? That was what I wanted to believe as I watched them all unfold their hands and sit back again on the pew. I had been still for the last few minutes, intent on studying the faces and the bearing of my family members. Apparently my decorum had pleased my mother, because she smiled at me and smoothed my hair and then whispered: "Do you know what? This is where your father and I got married."

I wasn't sure what to make of that information, though I knew it was significant, and it made the atmosphere of the cathedral even more charged and mysterious. I have a sense from old family photos what that wedding had been like: Bethie in her satiny bridal gown and Burt in his Army Air Corps uniform kneeling at a communion rail obscured by flowers, Vivian at her sister's side as maid of honor, everyone majestically dwarfed by the resounding floor-to-ceiling emptiness of the cathedral. But at that age I had never been to a wedding myself and had no way to conjure up a vision of one, so I was left with an impression of a colossally important event that could not really be seen or understood. Like the war that had brought my parents together, and myself and Danny into being, it was a hovering, shapeless thing.

"And the beast that I saw was like a leopard!"

The words came out of nowhere and for a few moments I couldn't tell who had spoken them. They had no connection to anyone immediately within sight, and because they were so amplified, disembodied, and echoing I wasn't sure they hadn't been spoken by God himself. It took a while for me to locate the source. The priest who had been standing at the altar with his back to us was now off to the side in a towering circular pulpit that resembled the battlement of a castle. He looked very small there. He had an unremarkable face and a plastered-down comb-over, but his green chasuble and his on-high presence more than compensated for his ordinary earthliness.

"It is this leopardlike creature that John the Apostle refers to in the Apocalypse," he went on. "And I suspect that for most of us here in Oklahoma City this week, the reference might be a little too close to home."

A discreet ripple of laughter emanated from the worshippers. It was a strange sound to hear in a place whose atmosphere was usually ruled by a crushing solemnity. But the escaped leopard had been on everyone's mind to begin with, and there was a collective relief at hearing something so immediately relevant mentioned out loud.

But that was as far into levity the priest was willing to go.

"And all the earth followed the beast in wonder," he went on, reading from Saint John's confusing fever dream again. "And they worshipped the dragon because he gave authority, and they worshipped the beast, saying, 'Who is like to the beast, and who will be able to fight with it?'"

The sermon that the priest gave was a chastening something about idolatrous folly, about the people of Oklahoma City allowing themselves to be hypnotized by the excitement of a beast let out of its cage. I remember being left with the frightening impression that the leopard was conflated with Satan, that they were in essence the same malevolent creature. And so whatever fear I had managed to shake off on this bright Sunday morning now came back with multiplying force.

The sermon ended but not the service. The Mass dragged on and on as it always did. When it came time for communion, Danny and I sat in the pew and watched as our mother and grandparents and Vivian walked up the aisle with their hands folded. Usually everyone but Danny and me—who were too young to participate in the sacrament—made the journey up to the communion rail. But this time Frank and Emmett stayed behind with us. I saw their nervous looks as they folded the kneeling rail and then sat back in the pew to allow others to pass. I was years away from learning that the fact that they were not going to communion meant that they were not in a state of grace, that they had committed sins that had not yet been expiated by going to confession. But I did understand that in that moment they must have considered themselves unworthy of receiving the host with the rest of the people in the church. Remaining seated during communion was essentially a way of proclaiming that you had committed a mortal sin. That was no doubt the reason for the looks on my grandparents' faces as they made their way out of the pew past Frank and Emmett. Big Dan's glance was one of anger and disapproval. Babi's was more complex—not just hurt and disappointment but a devout fear that if her sons died without confessing whatever sins were on their souls, they would go to hell.

Seated with Danny and my outcast uncles, I watched the procession of communicants up the aisle. This was the only part of the Mass that interested me, the chance to study a whole churchful of people as they paraded toward the communion rail in reverent silence. It was an opportunity to see and to understand that there were other families like ours, other families with children like us, children who had their own grandparents, their own mothers and aunts, their own restive uncles, their own unknown histories.

I noticed Frank nudge Emmett and then incline his head toward the aisle. He was calling attention to Hugh, who was part of the stream of worshippers making their way forward. Hugh walked behind a stout elderly woman with gray upswept hair that was covered by a transparent white mantilla. I knew intuitively, by the careful way he watched her steps, sometimes gently reaching forward to touch her elbow, that this must be the mother he had spoken about. As he passed our pew, he smiled and nodded in our direction, a gesture that included Frank and Emmett but that I understood was really directed toward Danny and me. Once more he seemed to be including us in his life, and ours in his, in a way that had not yet been explained to me.

I was worried that Frank would leap out of the pew and confront Hugh again, but he just nodded back in what seemed like a genial way. There was an ocean of things I didn't yet understand, and among them was why arguments arose in the first place and how they could be resolved or put on hold without any declaration. The rhythms of adult behavior were still silent and invisible to me.

"*Ite, missa est.*"

Those were the Latin words I had unconsciously trained myself to listen for. I didn't know that they translated as "Go, the Mass is ended." I only knew that when I finally heard them the ordeal of church was almost over.

It always took a while, once we had passed beneath the big stained-glass window at the back of the church and through the doors into the sunshine, to reach the car and get home and out of the Sunday clothes that tortured us. There were always people outside who wanted to talk to our grandparents, to put out their giant hands for Danny and me to shake and tell Bethie how they couldn't believe what handsome little boys we were and how big we had gotten. Among the greeters today were Hugh and his mother. He introduced her to us and, frail though she was, she crouched down to meet us at eye level and peer at us with sad and interested eyes. "Well, hello there, you two," she said, as if she had been looking around for us and had finally found us.

When she stood up again, I heard Hugh say to her, "And Mother, I'd also like you to meet Bethie's sister, Vivian, and her brothers, Frank and Emmett." My uncles stepped forward and shook her hand. To my continuing surprise Frank exchanged pleasantries with Hugh as if nothing had happened between them the day before.

We drove home, as we had come, in Frank's car. Emmett sat in the passenger seat and Bethie and Danny and I were in the back.

"Thank you," Bethie said to Frank.

"Thank you for what?"

"For not causing another scene."

"I told you I was sorry for that."

"I know you did."

"Maybe we could all just drop it," Emmett said. "Look, the Marines are out."

We were on Classen now, more or less on our usual route for our weekly Sunday drive heading toward downtown, as we passed a convoy of jeeps crowded with armed Marines in billed caps and fatigues.

Frank honked the horn and waved at them as he passed. "Keeping our country safe and secure from escaped leopards," he said.

"Oh, hush," Bethie told him. "You two were out hunting him yourself yesterday."

"It'll probably end up that nobody even shoots him," Emmett said. "He'll just starve to death. In the first place he's from India. And in the second place he's been living in a zoo. What does he know about how to hunt for food in Oklahoma?"

"Not much," Frank said. "But I bet you some lucky SOB is going to get him anyway."

He was silent as we headed toward downtown, following Big Dan's car with Babi and Vivian inside. After a block or two Frank made a U-turn around one of the traffic islands on the boulevard and headed back in the other direction, toward our neighborhood.

"I don't feel like driving by the Place today," he said. "I don't need him to rub my nose in the fact that I don't work there anymore."

"Stop bellyaching about it," Emmett said. "What else was he supposed to do?"

"Oh, so you're on his side now?"

"Stop this bickering right now," Bethie told them both from the back seat. Her tone was so firm and so familiar she could have been talking to Danny and me.

"Anyway," she told Frank, "we might as well go home. I have to get ready for work."

"I bet the hospital will be busy today," Emmett said. "A lot of people coming in for repair work after they tangle with that leopard."

"Or after they accidentally shoot each other," Bethie said, with a disapproving glance at a convertible filled with rifle-wielding teenagers. "I believe this whole city has gone insane."

13

When we got home, Danny and I were so anxious to get out of our Sunday outfits we almost ripped them off. The harsh wool fabric was suddenly so unbearable, now that the end was in sight, that I danced around the living room in torment like someone who had stepped in an anthill.

"Stop those theatrics!" Bethie said, as she held me still so that she could slide off my junior sport coat without me tearing off the sleeves. "I can't believe what spoiled children you are."

It didn't do any good for us to protest about our clothes, about what agony they were. She didn't care and she wouldn't listen.

"There are plenty of children," she said, with a logic that completely eluded us, "who would give anything to have such nice clothes."

She went into our room, opened the dresser, and returned

with two identical striped T-shirts and red short pants with elastic waists.

"I don't want to wear the same thing as Grady," Danny protested.

"I don't care what you want, young man. This is what you're going to wear."

"Why?"

"Because I'm your mother and I like it when you dress alike. What difference does it make to you?"

"What difference does it make to *you*?"

"Don't you dare talk back to me, Danny, or I'll give you a swat with the spatula. Is that what you want?"

She said this without any threatening inflections in her voice, so we knew she wasn't serious, just impatient. A little back talk was not a major infraction, not like ignoring her or even taunting her when she was already near tears after an exhausting day, or during the times—I realize now—when she felt vulnerable and lonely and was sunk in thoughts about the past and what she had lost. In any case, we didn't really fear a half-hearted swat or two from the metal spatula in the utility drawer. It was just something that we had agreed upon, for her sake, to pretend to respect.

She went into her bedroom to change clothes and came out dressed in her nurse's uniform.

"I want you boys to stay with your grandparents till I get back from work," she said, as she picked up her purse and surveyed the apartment, looking for last-minute things to tidy up. By that time Frank and Emmett had appeared at the front door. Part of the Sunday routine was for them to drive Bethie to her shift at the hospital, for Danny and me to go along, and then for our uncles to take us someplace like the zoo. But the zoo was closed today because of the leopard, so we were facing a long afternoon of staying at home.

Something else was different. I saw it in the way Bethie looked at her brothers as she walked with them to the car—or, more to the point, didn't look at them. Frank's hostile performance in my grandparents' living room the day before, his sloppy attempts during our bedtime last night to make it all right, and Emmett's inability or unwillingness to be anything other than complicit in his older brother's behavior: all this had visibly eroded her usual eagerness for her children to be at large in their company. But Danny and I argued plaintively enough that she agreed to at least allow us to ride along with them when they dropped her off at work.

We drove to the hospital in Frank's car, with Danny and me both squeezed into the front seat between Bethie and Frank, Emmett in the back staring pensively out the window. St. Anthony's was a towering Gothic edifice that would have filled me with foreboding if not for the fact that my mother worked there and came home from it every day without being harmed by it.

Frank wheeled into the circular driveway in front. Bethie kissed Danny and me goodbye and walked up to the entrance, her white nurse's uniform stark and crisp against the hospital's redbrick facade.

"Hold on a minute," Frank said to nobody in particular. He put the car in park, turned the ignition off, opened the door, and ran to catch up with Bethie, holding his hand over his chest pocket so his cigarette pack wouldn't be jostled out of it.

"Now what's he up to?" Emmett mumbled from the back seat.

"I don't know," Danny said.

"I know you don't, champ. I was just talking to myself."

We watched as Frank and Bethie stood under the front door portico. The car windows were open, but they were far enough away that we couldn't hear their voices. It was clear enough, from their body language, that Frank was trying to talk his sister into something. Bethie's arms were crossed. She wasn't looking at him, just staring at her left elbow as he talked. Gradually, though, she began to faintly nod, to uncross her arms, to speak while she held up a finger in front of her face, then finally to relax into a posture that signaled either agreement or capitulation.

Then she waved toward the car at us and went into the building.

"What was that all about?" Emmett asked Frank when he got back behind the driver's seat.

"Well, we're on probation, but she's going to let us have the boys for the afternoon, just like we always do. Have to keep up traditions, right?"

He turned to Danny and me. "Where do the two of you want to go? Can't go to the zoo, it's closed."

We yelled "Springlake!" in unison. That was the amusement park not far from the zoo where they had taken us on a few occasions. The park was built around the pastoral margins of a man-made lake that featured a lighthouse and miniature paddle-wheel steamer. There was a wooden roller coaster called the Big Dipper that we were too small to ride—although Danny had begged to—and a gigantic swimming pool with a water slide at one end and an enticing aquatic merry-go-round. The main draw for children our age was a fun house with bumper cars and distorting mirrors and ferocious blasts of air that would erupt at random times to lift up the skirts of startled women.

"Nope, Springlake is out," Frank said. "Your mother wants you to be indoors."

"Hugh took us to a movie," Danny said, after sulking for a moment.

"Well, hip-hip-hooray for Hugh."

"Easy," Emmett said.

"I know, I know. How about the state capitol? You boys ever been to see where the sausage gets made?"

We headed east and north of downtown, where the buildings of the state capitol complex stood among a scattering of working oil wells drilling into what was known as the Oklahoma City Field.

"That's the Petunia Number One," Emmett told Danny and me as we passed the largest of the derricks, which stood in front of the capitol building's parking lot. "That was the first one they drilled. When we first moved to Oklahoma City from Kansas, when we were kids, there were so many derricks that they were about all you could see from here to downtown."

"Like a big forest made out of steel," Frank said as he parked the car. "Most of it's gone now, but old Petunia there keeps drilling away. Now look, here's the deal. Your mother said you had to hold our hands till we get inside."

"The leopard doesn't attack in the daytime," Danny said, with a note of authority in his voice.

"Doesn't matter. You can't go running off. Neither of us wants to get into any more trouble with your mother."

"We might get the spatula," Emmett said.

The thought of Bethie chasing Emmett and Frank around the house the way she did with us, trying to swat them with a spatula, caused us to break out laughing. It was complicit laughter, though, a recognition that she was really the stern mother of not just two but four wayward children.

Hand in hand with our uncles we crossed the open plaza leading to the vast capitol building with its towering columns and porticos. At that age I had no idea of architecture, let alone Greco-Roman architecture, but the brute power of the exterior of that building, and the echoing emptiness we encountered when we stepped inside, introduced me to the idea of ancient time.

Up until then, the war had been my only temporal marker of the hazy gray void that had existed before my birth. Now I saw that the reach of that timeless world went far deeper, that this building had been standing here long before my parents, my uncles, my aunt, maybe even my grandparents had been alive, and that even this eternal-looking temple had once not existed, and that where it and the oil wells now stood had only been a frightening eternity of empty Oklahoma plains.

I may have been scared, or merely awed, as we climbed the stairways that led high up into the building. At that time the dome that had been originally planned for the capitol four decades earlier had still not been built, and a flat roof sealed off the upper levels of the rotunda. But the place was so big and I was so small that the distance from me to the ceiling was still overpowering. I looked up into what seemed like an entire sky trapped within a gray vault of granite and marble.

As I turned around in this space my attention gravitated toward a giant, turgid painting visible in a far alcove. Because it hung above the empty space of a stairwell, it was impossible to get a closer look, so I had to puzzle it out from a distance.

Beneath a sky full of boiling clouds a soldier in a steel helmet—flatter and lower than the helmets on my World War II vintage toy soldiers—said goodbye to his wife and baby while his parents, frail and gray and even older than Big Dan and Babi, stood sorrowfully to the side. And hovering in that busy sky was some kind of angel. She was not the sort of angel we were used to hearing about, the motherly Catholic angels with their welcoming arms open wide. This one had one arm upraised in martial resolve while the other arm gathered the American flag to her breast. On her head was a crested helmet. It seemed to me that she wanted to break up the sorrowful moment between the soldier and his family, to shame him into turning away from them and joining the other troops marching down the road in the distance.

I didn't like the angel, I didn't like the cosmic sense of menace the painting implied, and I didn't like the panels on either side of the main image, which depicted grieving female figures, their faces hooded, standing before massive monuments with names written on them. Even then I understood those must be the names of the dead.

This was not the same war from which my family was still emerging. Because of the soldier's strange helmet and the out-of-time clothing of his grieving parents, I could tell that this war belonged to an even more distant and mournful age.

"Look at that send-off," Frank said to Emmett as the four of us stood there staring at the painting. His voice echoed slightly off the marble floors. "Do you remember an angel coming down from the clouds when you said goodbye to Mom and Dad?"

"I remember Dad shaking my hand and Mom handing me

a rosary and a thermos of noodle soup. I was embarrassed to take the soup but I polished it off before the train even got to Tulsa."

He turned to Danny and me and gestured toward the painting. "That's World War One, boys. There weren't supposed to be any more wars after that one."

"Which is another of way of saying," Frank said, "don't believe anything anybody tells you."

We wandered around for another ten minutes, but it was a great empty building and there wasn't much to do except to register the impact of it on our small, insignificant selves. When we left the capitol Frank and Emmett grabbed our hands again, and we walked a hundred yards or so, past the oil wells to yet another imposing building with columns in the front.

This building, Emmett explained, as he pulled open a heavy steel door, was the state history museum. It represented our third visit today to a temple dedicated to unfathomable adult beliefs. Here, the thing being worshipped was history, which for all I knew was an assemblage of random objects haunted by disuse, much like the musty boxes of bygone things we had discovered in our grandparents' basement.

"Look at that, boys," Emmett said. He was directing our attention to a display case a few steps away from the entrance foyer. I peered through the glass at an assortment of underwhelming objects: old ledger books, certificates, a heavy pistol, a wooden stake, a blurry black-and-white photograph of people on horseback and in wagons racing through a cloud of dust.

Emmett crouched down next to Danny and me and pointed to a small brass bugle.

"You know what that is?"

"It's a horn," Danny said.

"Close. It's a bugle. And you know why it's special? It's because that's the bugle that started the Oklahoma Land Rush. It says here they played reveille on it."

We waited for an explanation, and Emmett seemed eager to fill us in. "That's how it all got started," he said. "It was like a big race, thousands of people lined up, waiting for that bugle to blow. Whoever got there first got the best land."

"Got where?" I asked him.

"Oklahoma. Right here where we're standing, it was nothing but empty land. None of this was here, no buildings or houses or anything. And then all of a sudden here comes this giant stampede of people all trying to stake their claim, to find someplace to live."

For the second time since we entered the state capitol complex, I was called upon to imagine an Oklahoma that had been empty and primordial. I had been born into a world that was there to receive me, born into something that had already been created, and that naturally seemed as permanent to me as the soil it was built upon. But I did my best to imagine a universe of blank wintry earth and desolate winds.

"It wasn't exactly empty, though, was it?" Frank said. His voice was loud. He had moved on from the Land Rush exhibit and was standing farther down the museum corridor, looking at another case, which contained beaded moccasins, rawhide shields, and deerskin breeches, and whose centerpiece was an imposing eagle-feather headdress like the ones I was familiar with from TV shows and from the bag of plastic cowboys and Indians that Bethie had bought us one Saturday at the dime store.

"There were lots of Indians here once," he told us, "and you know what happened to them?"

"No," Danny said.

"Killed them. Well, most of them. And then we brought in more Indians from the rest of the country because we wanted their land and dumped them here. Ever hear of the Trail of Tears? They ever talk about that on *Roy Rogers*?"

"Okay, Frank," Emmett said. "Don't get on your soapbox."

"Well, they ought to know the truth. If they want to know what this country is all about, what it was—"

He broke off when he noticed that other people in the museum were staring at him. Some of them were scowling.

"Aw, hell," he said, maybe to us, maybe to himself. We continued walking through the museum, past moldering buckboards and old butter churns and faded portraits of turbaned Cherokee chiefs. History was some sort of confused, corroded place, airless as a fish tank, a place where now-dead people had been held against their will, prohibited from entering the gleaming present.

As we continued to study the objects on display, Frank couldn't resist picking up his monologue, though he was aware of the other people now and was speaking only just above a whisper.

"America," he said. "Land of the free. Tell it to the Indians. Tell it to the draft board."

"Aw, come on, you weren't drafted," Emmett said.

"*You* were. And by the way, signing up was the dumbest thing I ever did."

He bent down to Danny and me.

"Don't ever volunteer for anything, you hear me? It's not worth it."

"Don't listen to him," Emmett told us. "He served his country and he's proud that he did his part, just like I am. In fact, anybody ever tell you that Frank won the Bronze Star and the—"

"Oh, quit your jawboning," Frank said. He was looking now at a display of cattle brands, looking at them but not seeing them, just staring ahead with his hands in his pockets. He took out his metal lighter and clicked the lid on and off. His agitation was building and I didn't understand what had triggered it. Was he really that upset about what had happened to those Indians long ago?

We went on touring the museum, but with a wary expectation that whatever we focused on next might set Frank off into another caustic downturn. There was a miniature child's stagecoach that Danny and I could climb in and out of, and as we did so our uncles sat down on a bench on the other side of the museum gallery.

I couldn't hear much of the conversation between them. There were a lot of visitors in the museum, and the high ceilings and marble floors created an echoing cacophony. But enough words came through that I understood it was the painting in the capitol that had set Frank off, and that continued to gnaw at him even now that we were in a different building among Indian relics and pioneer implements. I suspect that his resentment had something to do with the painting's all-enveloping patriotism, its assurance that the soldier at its center who was saying goodbye to his wife and baby and sorrowing parents would either die a noble death or come home as a conquering hero and settle into a steady life. As Danny and I sat on the driver's bench of the stagecoach, pretending to be the driver and the rifle-wielding deputy who guarded the strongbox, I kept straining to listen to the conversation between my uncles, waiting for it to return to the subject of their nephews, to provide some answer to the growing puzzle of what might lie in store for us.

But the voice I heard most clearly was neither of theirs. It came from the entrance hall, and it was so powerful in its outrage it cut through all the other recovering voices in the museum.

"No, we will not come back on Thursday!"

It was a male voice, defiant but nervous. When we looked down the corridor to the front of the building, we saw a Black man in a sport coat confronting the state employee on the other side of the reception desk who had greeted us when we had come into the museum. The employee, I could tell, was already in over his head. He was young and slight and had the recessive but righteous demeanor I've since learned to recognize as belonging to an inflexible species of rule follower.

The man confronting him was lean and wiry and middle-aged. He stood there with his feet planted and one hand grasping the elbow of his teenaged son, holding the boy in place so that he wouldn't run away in mortification or in fear. A crowd of museum goers had already gathered around them.

"Wait here," Frank called to us on the stagecoach as he and Emmett walked toward the entrance hall to see what was going on. I did what I was told and froze in place, but Danny didn't hesitate for an instant to disobey. He dropped down from the driver's bench and ran after our uncles, leaving me no choice but to follow.

By that time there were several dozen people clustered around the receptionist and the man and his son, and we were too small to see over any of them to get a clear idea of what was going on. We heard the receptionist as he kept talking about Thursday. Thursday was the day, he said, in his icy, overexplaining, cruelly courteous voice, when Negroes were more than welcome to visit the museum—but today was not that day, it was Sunday.

That wasn't enough of an explanation for the Black man in the sport coat. He kept arguing, and his outrage was gathering steam. The history of Oklahoma, he said, didn't just belong to white people. What was wrong about bringing his son here to give him a chance to learn a little something about the place they lived? It was bad enough that the zoo was also closed to Negroes except for one day a week, and was closed now in any case because of the escaped leopard. Yes, he knew that white people didn't want his son riding the roller coaster with their children at Springlake, he knew that they didn't want him sitting next to them in a movie theater. But come on, this was a museum!

As his voice kept rising, the circle of white onlookers kept massing tighter around him, and more people were now crowding in behind Danny and me, cutting us off from the view of what was happening not just in front of us, but behind us as well. We heard someone call out "Aw, go ahead, let him in," but he was answered by other voices who not only didn't share that opinion but were growing angrier and angrier at the presumption of a man who didn't know his place and wouldn't accept the rules.

We heard more shouting as the throng of people around us grew denser, an enclosing forest of adult legs. It was becoming dark where we were, as the bodies above squeezed out the light in the museum's entrance hall. I grabbed Danny around the waist—it was getting harder to breathe. Then I could guess from the sudden chaotic lurch of the crowd and a chorus of screams that a fight had broken out. It was harder and harder to keep our footing, but my survival sense told me that nothing was more important, since if we fell down it would go unnoticed and we would be trampled by all the adults pushing forward to see what was happening at the head of the crowd.

I heard Emmett's voice calling out "Danny! Grady!" but I didn't know what direction it was coming from. Then I saw what I thought were his trouser legs as he planted his feet against the packed-in bodies all around us, moving forward one hard-won step at a time like someone walking into a hurricane. In doing so, he caused another fight to break out above our heads, because the people who had been surging forward were now in a state of near-panic themselves as they were being pushed from behind. He ignored the enraged voices and flailing fists around him and managed to bend down, grab my brother and me by our armpits and wedge us inch by inch to the outer margins of the packed museumgoers, where we finally broke free and tumbled onto the marble floor, momentarily dazed by so much sudden light and air.

"I thought we told you to stay put!" Emmett said. We didn't have an answer for that, and before we could think of an excuse, he pulled us to our feet. Standing against the wall, outside the scrum, things didn't look quite so terrifying. It was almost comical, all those people straining and struggling to move forward, to get a view of the conflict that was supposedly happening ahead of them.

The crowd thinned as a guard opened the big double doors of the museum and the congestion spilled outside. Emmett led us there as well as soon as it was safe to pass through the doors. On the broad landing above the building's steps, there was room for the crowd to fan out and to get a glimpse of the focal point of the tumult. By this time, the Black man who had insisted on being allowed into the museum was giving ground in a strategic retreat, guarding his son while parrying attacks from two white men, one of whom was trying to pound his head with his fists while the other was grabbing his shirt.

And then we saw Frank. He was in the middle of it. I saw him reach with both hands and grab one of the white men by the shoulders and pull back so hard that both of them tumbled halfway down the steps. The enraged man was on his feet in an instant and he and Frank scuffled for a few moments more until two policemen rushing from the parking lot with their nightsticks pulled them apart. Two other policemen had arrived to do the same with the Black man and his remaining assailant and to bark orders for everyone to stand back.

There was a lot that I couldn't make sense of. Why did the police take the Black man and his son away and leave everyone else, all the white people, just standing there with no penalty or injunction other than to go on about their business? Why did Frank grin at and shake hands with the man he had just been fighting?

When Frank found us at the top of the steps he was still smiling. His shirt had been pulled out in the melee and he tucked it back in. He had a red mark on his cheek where he had been punched or slapped, but there was no blood, and overall he didn't look like someone who had just been in a fight.

"Well, what should we do now?" he asked Danny and me as if nothing had happened. "Want to see the rest of the museum?"

We both shook our heads. Going back into the museum seemed like an impossible thing to consider.

"I thought you'd have been fighting on the other side," Emmett told his brother, as the Black man who had insisted on being let into the museum was shoved into a patrol car by the police. "I thought you would have been against letting that Negro in."

"Well," Frank said, "he should have known better. He should have waited to come until Sambo Day. But if somebody wants to stand up for himself and not be told what to do, I'm on his side."

14

Frank was exhilarated by the scuffle that had just taken place, and as he drove away from the museum and the state capitol he kept rubbing the red mark on his cheek and working his jaw with a kind of satisfaction.

"Where to?" he called to Danny and me in the back seat. We should have been disturbed by the unexplainable thing that had just happened, but his lightheartedness short-circuited any lingering fear we felt and made it seem like it had all been just a game.

"Let's get in another fight!" Danny said. We were all suddenly giddy from the release of tension, and Danny and I began to pretend-fight, bouncing all around the back seat until we had squeezed ourselves up onto the rear-window ledge, where the horsing-around turned into aggressive tickling on Danny's part and then into something like a real fistfight.

"Hey! Hey! That's enough!" Emmett said. "Do you want me to have to come back there and separate you two?"

We didn't listen, or let up, so that's what Emmett had to do. He slipped over the front seat, extracted us from the window ledge, and sat between us, holding us each down with a powerful forearm.

"Stop somewhere," he called to Frank in the front seat. "Anywhere."

In those days, in those summers, there used to be places called watermelon gardens. They were temporary establishments that sprang up in June and closed down with the beginning of the school year. They sold only one thing, big lengthwise slices of watermelon for pennies apiece. You bought your slice and took it to one of a series of long picnic tables set out beneath the arborlike shade of an oak grove.

That was where we went next, one of these anonymous watermelon gardens somewhere on the eastern fringes of the city. The leopard was still on the loose, but the place was crowded with people who either had been hunting for the creature themselves or were driving around out of curiosity and excitement. The day was very hot, and the road leading to the watermelon garden was crowded with slow-moving safari traffic.

"I thought we had to be indoors," I said.

"It's all right," Frank said. "If your mother asks, tell her we were well protected."

He pointed to two young men standing at the gate that led into the establishment. They held rifles and wore white T-shirts that looked brand-new and had an image of a leaping leopard on the front, beneath a semicircle of words, a few of which were too unfamiliar for me to puzzle out.

"What does it say?" I asked Emmett as he lowered me to the ground.

"It says 'Oklahoma City Leopard Patrol.'"

"Somebody knows how to make a buck," Frank said.

He stepped up to a wooden counter and held up four fingers to a man wearing an apron streaked with watermelon juice and black seeds. The man reached into a tub, hefted a big Black Diamond watermelon onto a cutting board, and sliced it lengthwise into four sections with a butcher knife as long as a bayonet.

We took a seat at one of the picnic tables. The benches were sticky with watermelon juice. I stared at the slice of watermelon in front of me, which was almost as long as I was tall. We had been given forks. Some of our fellow customers were using them but others, like Frank and Emmett, just picked up their slices and gnawed away at the fruit, spitting out seeds and occasionally dabbing their faces with napkins.

"When she was your age, maybe a little older," Frank told us, "your mother could eat a whole one of these. When she was through you could see her belly poking out. It was about the same size as the watermelon inside it. That was in the Depression, back in Kansas. Forget about ice cream. Forget about Tootsie Rolls. If you wanted a treat, you pretty much had to make do with watermelon."

"Remember how good she was at Ping-Pong?" Emmett said to Frank.

"Who?" I asked him.

"Bethie. Your mother. She had this way of holding the paddle." He mimed a furious backhand. "She put so much power behind that hollow little ball she could knock your teeth out."

"Don't ever underestimate your mother," Frank said. He wiped some of the juice off his hands and walked over to the sales counter, where there was a metal water cooler. He came back balancing four paper cups of water between his interlaced fingers.

There was something about the look on Emmett's face as he watched Frank set the cups on the table. It was expectant and chastening at the same time.

"Maybe not a good idea," he said.

"Give me a break," Frank said. He took a silver flask out of his back pocket, poured something into Emmett's cup and then into his.

"You two don't get any," he told Danny and me.

"Can we have a coke?" I said.

"They don't sell cokes here," Emmett said. "And besides, you're going to be so full of liquid after you eat that watermelon you won't be able to hold anything else in those stomachs of yours."

"But you're drinking that," Danny told him, as he watched Frank screw the top back on the flask and put it back into his pocket.

"That's different."

"Why?"

"Because it has a neutralizing effect. Isn't that right, Emmett?"

"He's right. It neutralizes the watermelon juice."

We accepted this as if it made sense and went back to the enormous task of eating our watermelon. Frank and Emmett drank in silence. All of the tables that were under the shade of the trees were occupied, and the full force of the sun was bearing down on us, but they didn't seem to notice. They had shoved their own half-eaten watermelons aside and were watching us eat, smiling indulgently.

"Spit out the seeds," Emmett instructed. "You don't want a whole bunch of watermelons to start growing inside your belly."

"That's not true!" Danny said.

"It's true enough. If I were you, I'd be careful. Also, don't swallow bubble gum. They've found Egyptian mummies that had undigested bubble gum in their stomachs that was four thousand years old."

"Those are two cute little boys you have there," a female voice called over from a table a few yards away.

Two women were peering at us through their sunglasses and grinning through their bright red lipstick. They were young, in their mid-twenties at most, but of course that seemed old to me, and something about them seemed older still. The one who had called out had a raspy voice and a stylish blond pixie haircut that made her face loom large and intrusive.

"Adorable," agreed her friend. I liked the way she looked better. Her brunet hair was looser and her overall appearance was softer. She wore what I now recognize as capri pants and a sleeveless polka-dot top with a wide collar, and her bare shoulders were deeply sunburned and peeling.

"They're our nephews," Frank said, as he poured some more of the contents of the flask into his paper cup.

"I see you," the first woman said.

"See me what?" He was grinning at her and holding up the flask.

"Why don't you get those two poor little boys out of the sun? There's room over here."

She and her friend scooted over to make room on the bench, and the four of us left our table and walked over to theirs. The woman with the pixie haircut who had offered the invitation shook hands with Danny and me with mock formality and introduced herself as Beverly.

"And I'm Jennifer," her friend said. "Like Jennifer Jones."

"Jennifer Jones was born in Tulsa," Emmett said. "She's an Okie."

Jennifer looked at him with sudden delight. "Well, hello there, Mr. Movie Magazine!"

"My favorite movie of hers was *Song of Bernadette*," Beverly said. "And I'm not even Catholic."

"Don't get us started on being Catholic," Emmett told her.

"Oh? Why not? I think it's the best religion in the world because you can do whatever you want as long as you go to confession."

She turned to Danny and me. "Why aren't you boys out hunting the leopard?"

"Our mother won't let us," Danny said.

This occasioned great laughter from Beverly and Jennifer, for reasons neither Danny nor I understood. Frank and Emmett both smiled, perhaps proudly.

"Their mother is a serious customer," Frank said.

"Nothing wrong with that," Jennifer told him. "I don't think you boys have any business hunting leopards. There are kids with twenty-twos all over the place. Not much older than these two, hoping to get a shot at old Leapy. That's what the radio's calling him now—Leapy. Because of the way he leaped out of his cage."

"Maybe one of those kids will end up getting him," Beverly said, "and his mother will have a nice new leopard-skin coat. Good lord, what did you do to your face?"

She had just noticed the emerging bruise above Frank's jaw and reached out to tenderly stroke it.

"Does it look that bad?" he said, smiling at her.

Beverly and Jennifer insisted on knowing what had happened, and Frank and Emmett took turns telling the story of the scuffle in the entrance hall of the museum.

"That's terrible," Jennifer said. "I think colored people should be allowed to go anywhere and do anything they want the same as everybody else."

"That's right," Beverly said. "If it was up to me, and a Negro sat at my table where I work and wanted to order a hot roast beef sandwich, I wouldn't have any problem."

"If it was Willie Mays," Frank said, "I'd buy his lunch."

Beverly held out her hand, fingers waving, for Frank's and Emmett's paper cups. When they surrendered them, she reached under the table. I saw her pour something into the cups from a bottle she had concealed in a big purse. There was more laughter, and as the adults kept talking the laughter increased and their voices grew louder. Frank, though, at this stage of drinking tended to be careful with his words and watchful, which gave him a stillness that I could see interested the two young women. They both worked downtown, they said. Jennifer was a sales clerk at a jewelry store in the Colcord Building, and Beverly was a waitress next door at Beverly's Grille.

"That's right, my name is Beverly and I work at Beverly's Grille."

She turned to me and made a show of ruffling my close-cut hair. When she smiled, with her face close to mine, the smile was enormous.

"That's what's called a coincidence, honey. And it's a coincidence that is pointed out to me sixteen hundred times a day whenever a customer looks at my name tag."

"I bet a lot of customers look at your name tag," Frank said.

"Oh, aren't you sweet."

"We've taken you boys there," Emmett said to us. "It's the place that has that sign out in front of a chicken smoking a cigar and playing golf."

"That's because our best-selling dish is Chicken in the Rough," Beverly explained. She turned back to Frank. "Why do you think they call it that? It's only fried chicken."

"Rough is a golf term," Frank said. "So it makes sense in a way, I guess."

"Yes," Emmett said. "Whoever had the idea that a picture of a chicken playing golf would entice people into a restaurant was a genius. Also, have you noticed what the chicken is saying in the sign? 'I'd gladly be fried for Chicken in the Rough.' Well, of course he would. Who wouldn't?"

It took a beat for Beverly and Jennifer to catch the tone of Emmett's irony, but as soon as they did they exploded with laughter. Then there was more pouring of liquor into paper cups. Danny and I had eaten all the watermelon we could by then and we were growing bored and impatient, trapped in the bystander role of children watching adults get drunk.

At some point the bright summer afternoon began to change. The shade in which we sat grew darker, the temperature cooler. There was a steely intimation of a swift-moving Oklahoma thunderstorm. But nobody seemed to be paying much attention, and the storm still had not yet reached us when a woman began running through the watermelon garden. She was pointing up the road, where dozens of people had already gathered on a bridge.

"There he is!" she cried out in an agitated voice. "There he is! He's over there!"

"Who?" someone called back.

"The leopard!"

"Here we go!" said Frank, as he grabbed Danny's hand and Emmett grabbed mine. We all raced with the rest of the patrons toward the bridge. Beverly and Jennifer were laughing in excitement. Big raindrops had started to fall, and the women reached into their purses and tied plastic rain bonnets on their heads as they ran.

As soon as we reached the bridge, our uncles hefted us up against the concrete railing so that we could get a look at the leopard that supposedly had been located. There were a lot of people there now, but it was a long bridge and there was room for everyone to look out over a narrow, deep-banked creek. The banks were thick with scrubby trees whose interlaced limbs cast a deep shade over the strip of water below, making it look as gloomy as an underground stream.

People were pointing in every direction and yelling excitedly. The two members of the Oklahoma City Leopard Patrol had left their posts at the entrance to the watermelon garden and run along with everyone else to the bridge, where they stood at the railing, aiming their rifles at wherever the onlookers were pointing with the most enthusiasm.

"This is ridiculous," Frank said. "If there was a leopard down there he's long gone."

"Oh, really?" Beverly responded. She spoke in a thrilled, playful register. "Are you a big-game hunter or something?"

"Well, I have enough common sense to know that—shit, look at that sky!"

Everyone around us was still peering down into the creek

and the dark, congested banks on either side of it, but the tone of Frank's voice caused them all to look up and notice the thick cloud front that had already sealed the sky from top to bottom and had a malicious greenish tinge.

"Ladies," Emmett told Beverly and Jennifer, "I think it's time for us to say goodbye."

"Really?" Beverly's eyes were on Frank. I couldn't tell if she was pouting for real or just pretending to. "What kind of gentlemen would leave—"

"Beverly," Jennifer almost barked at her. "They can't stay here. They have the kids."

I saw Frank's own painful, apologetic smile as he said a silent goodbye to the two women and scooped up Danny again. Emmett did the same with me, and they ran with us down the length of the bridge and along the road, reaching Frank's Fleetline just before big pellets of hail began to bounce off the asphalt and off the car's roof.

"You hear that, boys?" Frank said, drawing our attention to the hail landing on the roof as he turned on the ignition. "Each one of those little plinks is a dollar sign. The body shop at your grandfather's dealership is going to be very busy. But you know what? I think I'll be taking my business elsewhere."

"Oh, shut up, there's a tornado coming," Emmett said.

"There's a tornado coming?" Danny said. I saw how wide his eyes were, not with fear but with excitement, and I did my best to control my own apprehension and match my expression to his.

"Don't worry, we're fine," Emmett told us. "We'll just call it a day and head back home."

He turned on the car radio but didn't turn the volume up high enough for Danny and me, in the back seat, to hear it above the sound of hail pounding the car and the squeak of the windshield wipers. But it was clear enough, from the look that they exchanged, that Frank and Emmett didn't like what they were hearing about the weather.

After a moment Frank turned the radio off and he and Emmett just studied the sky instead. The hail stopped in a little while as the traffic cleared on the road, and we managed to drive ahead of the storm front.

"You two keep an eye out in the back seat," Frank said. "Let us know if anything is chasing us."

"The leopard?" I asked.

"No, Grady, we're not worried about the leopard right at the moment," Emmett said.

In the front seat our uncles laughed about that, then Frank said to Emmett, "Sure hated to leave those two standing in the rain."

"I bet you did."

Frank looked over his shoulder and grinned at us.

"We made a big sacrifice on your behalf, you know? I hope you appreciate it when you grow up."

I don't know if they had been drunk before the weather turned, or—if they had been—whether they were still drunk now; but as we drove through downtown they grew more serious and concentrated. The great buildings looming above us looked different. Against the rich gray-green of the thunderclouds they had an almost living clarity, their borders so eerily precise that they looked like wooden puzzle pieces that had not yet been quite snapped into place. We passed Katz's drugstore, where the cat with the bow tie was still smiling. His stillness contrasted with the swirling sky around him and made him seem very nervous. It was a Sunday, and no one was downtown except for a few anxious-looking people scurrying down the street and disappearing into office doors. We drove by Chickasaw Chevrolet and I looked anxiously for Big Dan through the display windows. But the dealership, like many businesses back then, was closed on Sunday, and the Place was empty except for the new car models, which sat there as patiently as ever on the sales floor.

"Let's hope it makes it through," I heard Emmett tell Frank.

"Yeah, let's hope," Frank said. He sped up, though it was hard to know if we were still outpacing the storm, because by that time it was gathering itself all around us.

15

As we rode down Classen in the middle of the storm, the street's familiar landmarks appeared before me with supernatural force. The giant milk bottle on top of the package store was now blindingly white against the tumultuous atmosphere, and the neon fish that crowned Herman's seafood restaurant pulsed with the same electric urgency as the lightning bolts splintering the sky in the background. I knew these landmarks, these locations, but had a child's inability to link them together into a coherent mental map. I knew we were close to home but didn't know how close or how to get there. Usually this sense of spacial helplessness was just one more benign condition of childhood, but now I felt close to panic. Home was somewhere nearby, but if I had to find it on my own, I would have no more of a chance than a scurrying mouse.

Finally I recognized the drugstore that was the place where we turned off Classen onto our street. Before we reached the corner, we passed a kid riding a bike along the sidewalk. A lac-

erating rain was coming down, and the boy faced into it miserably. He rode hiked up on the pedals, cranking furiously against
the wind and rain. A sodden baseball glove hung by its strap
from one handlebar. I knew the boy, or at least had seen him
as we had driven past his house on our way to church or to the
zoo. He was often out on the lawn, playing catch with his father.
He lived on our street, two or three blocks farther east. He was
perhaps twelve, intimidatingly old and worldly to children like
Danny and me, with the freedom to roam at large through the
neighborhood on his red Schwinn. I had long admired this
bike: it had an intriguing red-and-white tank below the top tube
with a button on its side that, when pushed, sounded a horn.

"Jesus," Emmett said, looking back as the boy turned the
corner behind us. "What's that kid doing out in this?"

When we got to our house a moment later, Bethie was in
the front yard, home from work, waving her arms at us. She
had raced out from under the protection of the front porch,
where Big Dan and Babi and Vivian were all gathered. We
pulled up to the curb and she ran up and yanked open the back
door so hard that I thought she was going to tear it off.

"Thank God!" she yelled above the roar of the wind and the
thunder and the lightning that was now cracking all around us.
She pressed Danny and me against the sopping white fabric of
her nurse's uniform. "We've got to get to the basement! Now!"

She ran with us, still squeezing us against her body, up
the sidewalk to the front porch. I felt the hairs of my head lifting in response to the electricity in the air. We were all just
about to go through the front door and head to the basement
when Bethie turned and saw the boy who had been riding
home behind us standing in the middle of the street next to
his bike, looking around in confusion. I don't know why he

had stopped—maybe the effort of pedaling against the wind had proven to be too much, maybe he was just too scared to continue, or maybe he had made an informed judgment that he needed to find shelter immediately.

Bethie turned around and yelled at him from the porch.

"Honey," I heard her call against the roar of the wind, "come in here with us! Right now! Hurry!"

The word "honey" sounded strange when Bethie deployed it to speak to a boy who was neither Danny nor me. But it felt right too, the word that a mother would use to address any small frightened being. The boy couldn't hear her, but he saw her gesturing for him to run to her. He stood near the curb in front of our house, between the two tall sycamore trees that Big Dan had planted there long before we were born.

Bethie had just stepped off the porch to run to him when the world erupted with light. The sonic explosion that followed the lightning strike came almost immediately, but only almost. There was an opportunity, in that infinitesimal interval of silence, for me to study everything that was happening: my mother knocked backward to the ground; the weirdly precise shivering path the lightning bolt followed down the trunk of the tree; the way the tree split and threw out an obscuring shower of bark and branches and leaves; the boy no longer standing in confusion near the curb but lying still in the middle of our yard; and the red Schwinn whose handlebars he had been gripping now flung all the way to the opposite side of the street, where its front wheel spun in a slow, unconcerned way. I saw his black low-top Keds nearby as well. He had been blown out of them. They lay toe to toe on the grass as if they were having a secret conversation.

I thought at first that Emmett, who like the rest of us was

still standing outside on the front porch, had been knocked down by the blast in the same way that Bethie had. Then I realized he had just dived for cover behind one of the brick porch columns. Frank raced past him and bounded over the porch steps to Bethie. She was already in the process of getting up when he reached her and grabbed her arm and pulled her to her feet.

I knew she was all right by the way her voice rose above the storm. "Get him inside!" she screamed, pointing to the unconscious boy. Frank trotted over to where he was lying and bent down to pick him up. He moved so swiftly and decisively it seemed to me he was reacting to a moment he had been waiting and practicing for his whole life.

Emmett, though, was still a beat behind. By the time he had shaken off enough of the shock to help his brother, Frank was already on the porch with the boy and we were all headed through the front door. The whole family hurried to the rear of the house. Danny and I had been seized by Vivian, who held us by our wrists, taking no chance on just holding our hands and having us being able to wriggle out of her grip. She bore down so hard on my wrist that it felt like she was going to cut off the circulation to my arm, but I don't remember protesting. I could still hear the wind screaming outside, and the thunder that followed the lightning strike had had a concussive force that was still echoing in my head. I did not object to being painfully secured to an adult.

We went down the cement steps, back into the mildewy basement with its one bare light bulb where Danny and I had been the day before.

"Is he dead?" Danny asked as Frank laid the boy down on the concrete floor.

"Hush!" Bethie said.

I was awed by the tone of her voice. She was telling her sons, for the first time I could remember, that she had no time for us, that something more important had suddenly arisen and that we were in the way. I knew she was a nurse, but all that had meant for me in the past was the authoritative way she took our temperatures or applied Mercurochrome to our cuts or expertly held our jaws in her hands as she squeezed an eyedropper full of cod-liver oil down our mouths. Mostly it meant the disappointment of watching her going away for the day, away from us, to the hospital where she worked.

What was happening now was far different. She was in command. Her parents and her brothers deferred to her without a word as she pulled off the unconscious boy's T-shirt and put her ear next to his mouth.

"Wake up, honey!" she ordered the boy. "Wake up!" She shook him and then gave him a rap on the cheek with her open palm, but he didn't respond. His eyes were still closed, and in his helplessness he looked very small. He had a burr haircut. His hair was blond but so bleached by the summer sun it was as white as his bloodless face. All along his exposed chest and throat were strange red patterns so vivid I thought they were tattoos, though I know now that they were scars caused by the blood vessels the lightning had caused to rupture beneath his skin. In the moment, and in my memory, they were beautiful, a field of fernlike traceries that was hard to believe had not been applied by the hand of an artist.

"Let's turn him over," she said. Her voice was calm, but she was yelling because the wind outside was still roaring and there was now ear-splitting thunder all around us, and blasts of lightning illumination that made the small window at the top of the basement flicker like a TV set. Frank bent down and helped her turn the boy onto his stomach, then stood up and remained standing. He had his back to a big metal sink that Babi used for washing, and he was leaning against it with his hands on the rim.

Big Dan called out something that Frank either couldn't hear over the thunder, or in his lingering anger at his father chose not to hear. In any case, Big Dan rushed over and pushed him, so surprisingly and forcefully Frank almost lost his footing. He rebounded with his fists raised and with such a murderous look in his eyes that for a moment it looked as if the unthinkable was about to happen and my grandfather and uncle were going to get into a fistfight.

"What the hell?" Frank said.

"Do you want to get electrocuted?" Big Dan told him. "That's what'll happen if lightning strikes the outside water pipe that sink is connected to."

"For Christ's sake, you could have told me that without shoving me."

Whatever Big Dan said in response was lost in another blast of thunder that was simultaneous with another nearby lightning strike. No electricity was conducted into the basement, but it was enough of a demonstration of Big Dan's concern that Frank backed down and relaxed.

I doubt that my mother was even aware of this altercation. She was too focused on the unmoving boy in front of her. With a violence that startled me, she struck him on the back with the flat of her hand two or three times, then leaned over him and began administering, urgently but methodically, the version of artificial respiration that was in use back then, before mouth-to-mouth CPR became the standard. She pressed down on his back with her hands and her full weight, and then rocked back on her heels, lifting his helpless arms. She did this tirelessly and with rhythmic grace while thunder rocked the house above us and the family sat there watching her work to save the life of the boy.

Vivian was crying softly, asking every now and then—knowing that Bethie was too busy to answer but asking anyway—if he was going to be all right. Everybody else was silent. I looked over at Danny for some sort of guidance or reassurance, but like me he was too young to fully comprehend what was going on and just kept watching with frightful fascination as Bethie kept pushing down on the boy's back and lifting his arms by the elbows and then gently relaxing them. It was as if she were doing one of the exercises recommended by the jumpsuit-clad fitness experts I had seen from time to time on TV when there was nothing else to watch.

"Want me to spell you?" Frank asked, but she shook her head and just kept working. It was hot in the basement, and there was sweat pouring off the tip of her nose. The smell of mildew kept building as well, and the illumination from the single overhead light bulb and the small ground-level window grew dimmer as the unseen sky continued to darken. I knew the sensation of claustrophobia from occasional bad dreams, in which I was aware of some formless thing, some atmospheric menace, gathering to attack me, to smother me in my bed. I looked around the basement and thought at first that Emmett was gripped by the same sort of nightmare. He looked much the same as he had when we had crept up the stairs that night to the garage apartment and encountered him paralyzed by dread. Now he was staring ahead, shivering even though the air in the basement was oppressively humid. Every time there was a house-rattling burst of thunder he didn't just flinch like I did but withdrew farther into a kind of desperate passivity. I had seen that posture before, on some nature show Danny and I had watched on TV. A lion had seized an antelope and was holding it by the throat. The antelope squirmed frantically at first but then stopped, alive for the moment but somehow sensing the need to stop moving, to remain still and compliant in the lion's jaws.

Babi, standing at the foot of the basement stairs, watching Bethie perform artificial respiration on the stricken boy, shifted her eyes to Emmett. She saw what was happening to her son and lowered herself to the floor beside him, smoothing the dress over her wide hips, moving painfully on stiff knees. Emmett didn't object when she reached over to him with both arms and pulled his head onto her shoulder. For a moment, none of us seemed to have noticed that the fast-moving storm had passed, that the sky was brightening through the little window, and that it was now quiet enough that we could hear the boy's first shocked, gasping breath.

"Turn over, honey," Bethie told him as she helped him onto his back. He looked around him with wide-eyed alarm at all the strange faces gathered together in the basement staring down at him, and he began to sob with confusion.

"It's all right, sweetie," my mother said, stroking his forehead. She was crying softly herself. "You're all right now. You had a little accident but you're just fine. You couldn't be better. What's your name?"

The question set off a wave of panic in the confused kid. He looked down at his feet, at his rain-drenched white socks.

"Where are my shoes?" he screamed.

"I know where they are!" I said. Everyone looked at me.

The fact that I could say something useful gave me a surge of pride. "They're lying out there in the yard."

"I'll get them," Big Dan said. "Everybody else stay here. There may be power lines down."

He went up the stairs and came back a few minutes later with the shoes. The laces were still tied. The boy took the shoes from Big Dan and untied them and put them on his feet and tied the laces again while trying to keep himself from crying but not succeeding. Emmett was calmer now. Babi was no longer holding him, but he kept staring ahead without looking around. I knew that he didn't want anyone to see him.

"It's safe to go upstairs," Big Dan said. "There's some trees down but the tornado seems to have missed us."

The boy had recovered enough to walk up the stairs with Bethie guiding him, and to sit in the breakfast room while Babi made him and Danny and me Ovaltine. He had put his T-shirt back on and the strange patterns on his body were covered, but I could still see some of the scar tendrils on his upper arm. I heard the adults in the other room whispering to each other in the kitchen about whether they needed to call an ambulance or take him the hospital. Bethie said it would be better if his parents took him, though he still hadn't told anybody his name. But in a few minutes he said, unprompted, that his name was Anthony Wooten and that he lived at 1452 NW 34th Street, and his phone number was JA-41866.

Our phone number was JA-41940. I've remembered it all my life, and sometimes I've had dreams that if I could only find a rotary phone and could dial that number it would activate some sort of time machine and I would be magically transported back to that time and to my childhood household in Oklahoma City. But in the moment, when the boy recited his phone number with the same assurance with which I had been taught to recite mine, I felt jealous, robbed of the illusion that the JAckson telephone exchange was something that belonged to me and my family alone.

Big Dan picked up the phone receiver but there was no dial tone. The lines were down.

"Come on, Anthony," he said. "I'm going to take you home."

"I better come with you," Bethie said. "I want to keep an eye on him."

Big Dan nodded at her. I saw the pride in his eyes at what his daughter had just done. The boy said nothing, just followed Big Dan and Bethie out the back door to where the car was parked.

"Well," Vivian said to Danny and me after they left. "Are you boys aware that your mother is a hero?"

I was aware. There had been something thrilling about watching her in action from the moment she had picked herself up from the ground after the lightning struck. I had often seen her beset with worry or mute with grief; I had seen her overreacting when she snatched us out of the park when the news came that the leopard was on the loose. But I had never seen her in command, never witnessed what she would have been capable of during the war, or the kind of things she did every day in the hospital when she left us at home with our grandparents or Vivian or our uncles.

"You should have seen that boy's parents when we brought him home," Big Dan said when he and Bethie returned a half hour later. "You should have seen the look in their eyes when I told him that my daughter had saved his life."

"Oh, don't be silly, Daddy," Bethie said.

"What are you talking about? You saved his life!"

We were all out in the front yard, where Danny and I had put ourselves to use picking up some of the small branches that the wind had stripped from the trees and that now littered the yard. Big Dan had heard on the radio that three tornadoes had hit Oklahoma City, one of them plowing through downtown. He drove off again to see if there was any damage to the dealership. Babi went into the house to cook dinner while the rest of us lingered outside, cleaning up the yard in the intoxicating after-storm clarity of the evening.

"I suppose I'd better go in and help Mother," Bethie said. But she didn't go anywhere. She just stood there for a moment more and then rushed over to Danny and me and seized us both in her arms and started to cry. This might have embarrassed me on another occasion, but not tonight. The love of my mother was a feature of my world that I never gave a thought to. It was as powerfully present but unremarkable as the ground we stood on. There had been no beginning to it, there was no possibility it could ever be withdrawn. But tonight I was aware, maybe for the first time, that I was privileged to be the recipient of it. I had been jealous when she had called that stricken boy "honey," and the fact that she had saved his life had made her seem for the last hour or so oddly distant, a person who belonged not just to Danny and me anymore but threatened to belong to the whole world.

She wiped her eyes and looked up at Frank, noticing the bruise on his face for the first time.

"How did you get that?"

"I don't know," he said, putting his hand to his jaw. "Maybe something hit me when the lightning struck."

She walked over to inspect the bruise. "Well, it doesn't

look too bad. A little swelling. Where were you all when all this started?"

"We took the boys to the capitol and the history museum," Frank said. "And then we ended up at some watermelon place. The storm started to come on and we got out of there."

"Thank you for getting them home safe," she said.

"Sure." He glanced at Danny and me, just enough of a look to let us know that he knew we were there. We understood that maybe it was best that we didn't say anything about the fight that had broken out in the museum.

Emmett didn't say anything, either. He was hauling the metal porch glider from the driveway where it had been blown off back to the porch. His silence registered to me as shame, though I didn't understand what he might have been ashamed of. I suspect it might have had something to do with the knowledge that he had allowed himself to drink away part of the afternoon in the presence of two strange women with his nephews sitting there cluelessly watching. Or just as likely it had been the more acute episode when he had lost control of himself again after the lightning strike, ending up in the comfort of his mother's arms just like Danny and I were now.

"Here comes Mr. Wonderful," Vivian said. She shifted her eyes to Frank. "You be on your best behavior, or after I'm through with you you'll wish you'd been struck by lightning."

Frank gave a grim little laugh in response as Hugh pulled up to the curb in his light-blue Oldsmobile. Because my grandfather was a Chevrolet dealer, I had formed the impression that every other make of car represented not just a competitor but a foreign threat. But I couldn't take my eyes off the hood ornament of Hugh's enemy car—a stylized chrome jet that was far more imposing and elegant than the cursory hood ornaments that Chevrolet produced. It was so sleek and aerodynamic it seemed to me it was pulling the car behind it.

Hugh got out of the car and walked onto the lawn. I could tell he wanted to rush over to Bethie, but he had the judgment not to, and to address everyone at once instead. He said he was glad to see everyone was all right and wanted to know if we needed anything.

"A boy got struck by lightning," Danny blurted out, "and my mother saved him!"

"What?"

He shifted his eyes to Bethie. She had stopped crying, but her eyes were still red and all the adrenaline that had built up while she was trying to revive Anthony Wooten, and that had now been discharged, made her body look wobbly and slack. Hugh resisted the temptation to reach out to her, just listened with growing admiration while Danny described what had happened, with Vivian or Frank filling in the details while Emmett looked down from the porch, still emotionally wrung out in his own way.

"They said the lightning knocked you down as well," Hugh said to my mother when the story had been told. "Are you sure you're all right?"

"Sure I am. I'm fine."

Hugh stared at her for a moment, then smiled and shook his head in amazement, then looked at us.

"What do you boys think about your mother?" he asked.

I shrugged, not knowing what to say, not wanting to share what I thought about my mother with Hugh. Danny did the same.

"I think you must be pretty proud of her," he said.

"She knows her business," Frank said.

"That she does." Hugh and Frank were being pleasant with each other, but there was still something between them, something invisible but palpable, like the static electricity I had felt before the lightning strike.

"How is your mother, Hugh?" Bethie asked him.

"Oh, she's lived in Oklahoma all her life. She was calm as could be, down there in the basement listening to a Bing Crosby record. I doubt she would even notice a tornado unless it blew her house away."

He asked if there was anything he could do to help, haul away some brush or run to the store. But there was nothing that needed doing.

"Well, just wanted to check to make sure everything was all right," he said. He still had his car keys in his hand.

He was about to turn to leave when Bethie walked over to him, kissed him on the cheek, and thanked him for coming.

We watched as he drove away, the pale-blue paint of his Oldsmobile gleaming almost supernaturally in the fading light.

Emmett came down from the porch, put his hands in his pockets, and looked up at the sky. It was almost dark now. He spoke for the first time since we had come out of the basement.

"I wonder what that leopard thought of the storm. Out there in the open all by himself."

"He wasn't listening to any Bing Crosby records," Frank said.

"Good lord, we forgot about the leopard!" Bethie said, grabbing my hand and then Danny's and hauling us back into the house before the creature we had momentarily neglected to fear could spring out of the dusk.

16

"Who wants to go to the Place with me and help with the damage?" Big Dan said the next morning at the breakfast table in my grandparents' house. When I looked over at the newspaper on the table beside him, I saw a big dark photo of a tornado and, below that, part of a headline that featured the word I had learned to recognize more than any other in the last few days: "Leopard." I was too preoccupied with the photograph and headline I was looking at to answer Big Dan's question.

"Did they catch the leopard?" I asked him.

"No, not yet," he said, picking up the newspaper and unfolding it. "It says here 'Rough Night for OKC Leopard.' All the other animals were safe and cozy in the zoo, but he was out there somewhere dodging tornadoes."

"Poor thing," Babi said. "He was probably scared to death."

"Well, maybe he's had enough adventures and is ready to come back to the leopard pit. It says here they've left some doctored horsemeat out for him."

"What's doctored horsemeat?" Danny asked.

"Leopard food. They put some medicine in it. If the leopard eats it, it'll put him to sleep, and back he goes into the zoo and nobody has to shoot him. Or shoot each other looking for him. So—who's going with me?"

We eagerly announced that we were, and Babi told us to hurry up and finish our cereal. Bethie and Vivian were both there finishing their own breakfast, Bethie in her nurse's uniform and Vivian dressed for her office work in heels, a slim-fitting beige suit, and a hovering cloud of perfume.

"You'd better drop me off too," Bethie said.

"I thought Frank was on Florence Nightingale duty," Vivian said.

"Frank's not up yet," Bethie told her. "Neither is Emmett. So somebody else needs to drive me."

I could see the familiar tightness coming over Big Dan's face. Bethie saw it too.

"Daddy," she said, in a cautionary voice. "Let them sleep."

"Emmett has a job he has to get to, and Frank has only one job at the moment, which is to drive other people in this family to work."

He put down his napkin and walked out of the room and through the kitchen and out the back porch before any of the three women in his presence had a chance to try to dissuade him. Babi just looked at her two daughters and shrugged.

"Things are hard on him right now," she said.

He was back in five minutes. There had been no confrontation, at least none that any of us witnessed. It was plain, even to me, that all he had done was walk down the driveway and climb the steps to the garage apartment and pound on the door and try to get his two grown sons out of bed, with no success. But it was an effort he had needed to make, for the sake of his own pride if for nothing else.

"All right," he said when he came back into the house. "All aboard."

We dropped Bethie off first at the hospital, and then Vivian at the downtown office building where she worked. From the curb, we watched our aunt walk down the street with a crowd of other men and women dressed in stylish business attire. Several of the women turned to greet Vivian and broke into a rapid-fire conversation on their way to the front door, laughing and gesturing and then—when she pointed out her nephews in the car—waving at us with sudden delight. It was incomprehensible to me why they were so glad to catch a glimpse of us, but at the same time it was something I expected. I was a little boy, so why shouldn't I be adored? One of the women turned to Vivian with a mock frown.

"That's not fair," I heard her say through the rolled-down window. "They're too cute!"

"Don't I know it!" Vivian told her, and then disappeared through the revolving door of the building.

Vivian looked like she had a lot more fun at her job than our mother, who always arrived at work in a starched white uniform and mingled on the way in not with fashionable secretaries but with nuns in black habits that hid everything human except for their circumscribed faces. But I knew—especially now—that what she did at the hospital every day was gravely important.

We climbed into the front seat with Big Dan after we dropped Vivian off. Chickasaw Chevrolet was only a few blocks away, but instead of taking us straight there he pulled the car over to the curb and tapped the steering wheel for a few moments like he was trying to think of what to say.

"I want to talk to you boys a minute," he finally said. "I'm not going to pretend I know anything about what anybody else has gone through. Who knows what would have happened to me if I hadn't caught the flu in 1918 just before we were supposed to ship out? But there's something in life called responsibility. That's when you do what you're supposed to do; you don't just say you'll do it—you do it. I want you boys to remember that. Sometimes life is easy, sometimes it's hard.

"I know they both had a rough time over there," he went on. I understood now that he was talking about our uncles, and I thought I understood that "over there" had something to do with the war, but it was strange to hear him speaking this way, like he was talking to himself and not to us. "I'm not saying your uncles aren't heroes. I'm not saying I'm not proud of them. But they've still got to get up in the morning and get on with their lives.

"Your father," he said. "He had some rough times too. Got shot down himself, saw plenty of his friends get shot down as well. Most of them didn't survive that like he did. Most of them didn't come back from the war. But he did, and he gave us you two boys. I wish you could have known him."

He was staring down the street over his steering wheel, not looking at us.

"Do you boys miss having a father?" he asked.

We said we didn't. As far we knew, that was the truth.

"Well, we're all trying to do the best we can for you. The best we can for your mother. And your uncles are doing their best too. They just have to get in gear. You understand?"

We nodded cluelessly, and he pulled back out onto the street. As we drove along, we could see workers at various downtown businesses sweeping up glass and boarding up broken windows.

"Looks like the tornado tore up Walker pretty good," Big Dan said, "and then it must have made a left turn here onto West Main somehow."

He turned onto West Main as he said this, and up ahead we could see the blown-out showroom windows of Chickasaw Chevrolet. Big Dan didn't park in his usual space behind the building. He parked across the street and placed a protective hand on each of our shoulders as we walked over, telling us to watch where we put our feet so that we didn't step on any broken glass. He was greeted by a half-dozen employees all talking at once and guiding him through the ruined showroom, where one of the cars on display, a Styleline Deluxe station wagon with wood trim, had a smashed windshield and a deflated tire. The wind had also ripped down the Dinah Shore poster. She stared up from the floor, still smiling, as if nobody had told her what had happened to her.

Big Dan listened to what everyone was saying, took it all in calmly, asked a few questions, gave some orders that sounded more like suggestions, and then took us up to his office. He hung his fedora on the hat rack inside the door and told us to stand at the window and watch the crew at work putting the showroom back together.

"We'll be open again in two hours," he predicted. "It won't look quite as pretty with all the plywood everywhere, but we'll be back in business."

Maybe that was what was behind his thinking for bringing us there, so that we could witness a living demonstration of bouncing back from adversity. I had noticed how, while we were waiting out the tornado in the basement, he had stared at the wall instead of looking at Emmett as he shook with terror in his mother's arms. He hadn't seemed callous, just unready or unequipped to face a helplessness in his grown son he might not understand.

"I've got my two grandsons here," he announced proudly over the phone to someone he was speaking to, a factory manager or an insurance representative, before launching into a crisp and unemotional damage report. He winked at us while he talked, performing for us maybe. He hung up, punched a button at the base of the phone, picked up a waiting call—some emergency from the service department—then hung up and took another call from another department and told whoever it was to "hold your horses." It was bewitching to watch our grandfather in action, secure in a world he commanded, amid contingencies he could control.

But there were other contingencies for which he couldn't be prepared. I knew that as soon as I looked down from his office window and saw Frank entering the showroom, greeting his former coworkers, shaking hands all around, then picking up the Dinah Shore poster off the floor and grabbing a stepladder so that he could hang it back up on the wall where it belonged.

"There's Frank!" Danny called out.

"What?" Big Dan said.

He was about to punch another button and make another call on his phone, but he put the receiver back into the cradle and walked over to the window. He watched Frank at work on the top of the stepladder, reapplying rubber cement to the poster and smoothing it back into place.

"Wait here," he told us.

He left the office and then reappeared in the window as he entered the showroom below. We couldn't see his face but the employees who could seemed to regard him with concern as he made his way to Frank, who was just stepping down from the ladder. Big Dan said something to him, and we saw Frank gesturing around at the littered showroom in response. He was smiling and calm, but there was something provocative about that calmness.

As usual, Danny wasn't about to stand there and do what he was told. I followed him as he ran out of the general manager's office and down the stairs. We stood there at the entrance to the showroom, watching from what we thought was concealment as Big Dan took Frank's elbow and guided him away from the rest of the employees to a corner of the room. As they walked, I could hear broken glass crunch under their oxfords. Frank wore a dark-blue sport shirt with a pale-blue collar. Big Dan wore a suit, as he always did when he was at the Place. I didn't have an eye for tailoring then, and still don't, but I remember thinking of that suit as drab and shapeless, and—projecting from my own sartorial church experience—a misery to wear. Nevertheless, it gave him an on-duty appearance that added to his sense of authority. Next to him, Frank looked underdressed and diminished.

We heard their conversation. Big Dan asked Frank, not so much in anger but in genuine puzzlement, what he was doing here. Frank said that Chickasaw Chevrolet had been his place of work, that the people employed there were, for the most part, his friends, and he didn't see what was wrong about him volunteering to help them out when they could probably use an extra hand. He kept his voice low and steady, but

I could sense how he was using his logic as a weapon against his father, forcing Big Dan into a place where his objections would seem unreasonable. They weren't having an argument, but they weren't having a discussion, either. It was like something out of the soap operas Vivian watched on TV—two adults speaking in a way that seemed normal, but you could tell by their clipped voices and their flat stares that they weren't really talking about what they appeared to be talking about, that there was something dark and ominous infecting the conversation.

I was expecting another confrontation, but it didn't come. Maybe this was because when Frank shifted his eyes over to the stairway he saw Danny and me standing there listening. With a nod in our direction he got Big Dan's attention, and the tension between them slackened. Neither of them wanted to have another fight in front of us.

They talked for a few minutes more, though they were talking so quietly now that I couldn't hear them. Big Dan nodded from time to time in a way that seemed conciliatory. Frank stood above him—two or three inches taller. He rested his hands on his hips as he slowly shook his head, and several times he lifted his arms and made a gesture with his upturned palms, a gesture that projected—as I process it now—an attitude of facetious confusion.

They probably came to some sort of compromise, because Frank ended up hanging around for an hour or so, continuing to clean up alongside his former coworkers, making whatever point about his continuing relevancy he was trying to make. While he was working, Big Dan took us back up to his office, and we continued to listen to him talk on the phone while we watched the repair work going on below through the big window.

When Frank appeared at the top of the stairs, Big Dan told whoever he was talking to on the phone to hold on a minute and turned to Danny and me. "Your uncle Frank is going to take you boys out to lunch and then take you home."

That must have been part of the agreement that had been reached between them. It was fine with us. Watching people sweep up glass and put up plywood had turned out to be boring, but going somewhere with Frank always reinforced the prospect that life had the potential to be exciting.

17

The linkages that connected one event to another were mostly invisible to me, as I suspect they are to most young children. When I think of myself during that time, one of the things that come to mind is a book Bethie used to read to us, in which the image of a grasshopper was attached by some sort of spring to the binding. When she turned a page, the grasshopper would land on it, with a slap that was almost as violent as the closing of a mousetrap.

Like that grasshopper moving from page to page, I felt myself moving from one place or moment to another with the same conclusive whap. I was somewhere, then—for reasons that were rarely explained to me—I was somewhere else. I had no complaint about this. Children are passengers, always being moved here and there at adult whims and through adult means. But the sense of having no volition of my own, and no real sense of how one thing led to another, infused my existence with a never-ending air of mystery and made the logical developments that adults had set into motion seem like super-natural events.

That was how I reacted when Frank took Danny and me out to lunch that day and the waitress who greeted us broke into a broad smile. "Well, look who just showed up at my table!"

It was Beverly, the woman we had met at the watermelon garden the day before; and we were in Beverly's Grille, the downtown diner she worked at and shared her name with. Danny and I looked at each other in astonishment. It could not have occurred to us at our ages to think that this reunion was anything other than a world-shaking coincidence.

But of course Frank must have been thinking ahead. He was already downtown, he had been assigned the task of taking his nephews out to lunch, and he knew where Beverly worked. And he probably suspected that having Danny and me in tow would help shield him against any perception of being too forward or too eager to see her again.

"I was curious to see if you'd be open," Frank told her, "after that tornado yesterday."

"Oh, I thought you might be curious to see whether or not I was alive."

"That too."

She laughed as she passed out menus. She said there had been no damage at all. The tornado had skipped down Main Street, knocking over cars and breaking windows, but it had jumped up before it had gotten to their end of downtown.

"It was a terrible storm, though," she said. "Good thing we all got home okay."

She took our orders—halibut fingers for Danny and me and a hamburger for Frank—and winked at us and left.

"That's the same lady we saw yesterday!" Danny whispered in wonder to Frank.

"Ever heard the expression 'It's a small world'?" Frank said.

"No."

"Well, it is, and we just proved it."

In a little while Beverly came back with our plates.

"The freshest halibut in Oklahoma City," she said when she put our dishes of frozen fish in front of us. "Caught it myself this morning in Lake Hefner."

She turned to Frank and squinted a little, making a show of inspecting the mark on his cheek he had gotten in the fight at the museum.

"Your face is looking a little better today."

"You're just getting used to it," Frank said.

Flirting was an unknown form of interaction to me, but I could feel how the two of them had sealed themselves off into their own cocoon of conversation. Maybe it was because I felt excluded that I decided to breathlessly inform this woman that my mother had saved a boy's life.

"Is that right, sweetheart?" She looked at Frank again. "Your—"

"Sister," he reminded her.

"Your sister saved a boy's life?"

"She's a nurse!" I blurted out.

"We're proud of her," Frank said.

"I should say," Beverly told him. "You'll have to tell me about it sometime."

"I just might."

"Well," she said. "I better get back to my labors of Hercules."

She reached out a hand and touched Frank lightly on the shoulder.

"You're a good uncle," she said.

He said he tried to be, and she walked off smiling.

"Guess we'd better leave her a good tip." Frank said this to us, but his head was turned, watching her as she took the order from another table.

As we left the restaurant on the way to our car, I saw two men exiting the door of a building a block away. One wore a suit, the other a safari jacket. The man in the safari jacket carried a rifle and was in animated conversation with the man in the suit. They were both so dazzlingly familiar to me that I stopped and stared in disbelief. It had never occurred to me that the people I saw trapped within the TV screen were, or even could be, actual people. But here they were, catapulted onto this downtown sidewalk, into my own real life: the familiar TV announcer and the big-game hunter with the bullet-shaped head who had warned us about the man-eating leopard of Rudraprayag. It was as if 3-D Danny himself had materialized in front of me.

I grabbed hold of Frank's arm and pointed in their direction, almost unable to speak. Danny had the same reaction. Neither of us knew that the TV station from which they had been broadcast into our homes was just down the street from the restaurant where we had eaten lunch.

"Well, look at that," Frank said. "The leopard expert himself. Let's go talk to him. Maybe we can get some tips."

The two men were getting into a car as Frank hurried over, with us trailing behind.

"Hey there!" he said to the big-game hunter. He held

out his hand and introduced himself. The man returned the handshake but said nothing. The announcer—the man in the suit—who had just now opened the driver's-side door looked annoyed.

"The two of you off to bag that leopard?"

"Naw," the announcer said. "We're going to lunch."

Frank ignored him, speaking instead to the hunter. "Okay, but after lunch: any particular place you're thinking of searching? Any part of the city you recommend to my associates and myself?"

The hunter half-smiled and shook his head in exasperation when he looked down at Danny and me, Frank's "associates."

"I recommend you just stay at home," he said. "There's too many people out there already who don't know what they're doing. And kids—" he addressed this directly to us—"that leopard is dangerous. You should tell your father to get you back indoors right now."

"Uncle."

"Excuse me?"

"I'm their uncle, not their father. And yeah, they know the leopard is dangerous. They've been having nightmares about him, thanks to you."

"Don't pin that one on me, pal. I'm just telling the truth."

"Yeah, okay," Frank said. He turned to Danny and me. "Guess we better let these big-time TV stars go to lunch."

The hunter replied to this comment with a contemptuous wave and got into the car. We watched them drive off.

"'Too many people out there who don't know what they're doing,'" Frank said, repeating the hunter's dismissive comment. "Yeah, like that guy really knows anything about leopards. He probably just read an entry about them in the encyclopedia and now he's a world-famous expert. I'll guarantee you—whoever it is who shoots that leopard, it's not going to be that guy."

He led us back down to where our car was parked. As we passed Beverly's Grille, he waved to Beverly through the window. She smiled but couldn't wave back, because she was carrying a heavy tray with both hands. Despite the sour interaction with the two men from the TV station, Frank was in a buoyant mood, a better mood than I would have expected after we left Chickasaw Chevrolet. He had come into the dealership with some sort of confrontational agenda and had driven away not saying much, with a grim, defeated look on his face. But now he had recovered his spirits.

"Let's go roust your deadbeat uncle out of bed," he said.

When Frank pulled into the driveway in front of the garage apartment, we followed him through the door that led past our apartment and up the stairs with its pungent rubber runners. Emmett was awake but not fully dressed, wearing an undershirt and pants but no socks or shoes, eating a bowl of cornflakes. He had not combed his hair yet, and it was all skewed over to one side of his head in a way that made it look like it could throw him off-balance. Hanging on the wood-paneled wall behind him was a framed forest landscape that had always fascinated me. Its sketchy lines and muted colors had been part of the implanted decor of my world since my consciousness first began to emerge, and to me it represented the same swampy nothingness that I imagined had existed before my birth. I didn't learn until much later in my life that Emmett, and not some long-dead artist, had painted it.

"I hope you called in sick, at least," Frank told him. "You don't want to piss off your boss like your big brother did and be out on the streets."

Emmett just gave him a look and told him not to say "piss off" in front of us. Danny made his way to the pool table and stood on tiptoe so he could roll the balls around. I slumped back on Emmett's unmade bed and watched. I felt comfortable there, in the place above our own apartment where our uncles lived their adult lives. After a moment I walked over and picked up Emmett's cereal box. On the front was a picture of a big ear of corn and below it black-and-white photos of two bald-headed old men.

"Who are they?" I asked.

"Eisenhower and Stevenson," Emmett said. "They're running for president. Which one do you think we should vote for?"

"I don't know."

"I'll tell you a secret," Frank said. "It doesn't make one bit of difference which one anybody votes for. They're both politicians. And there they are on a cereal box just like Tony the Tiger. Shows you how low this country can go."

"I don't want to talk about politics," Emmett said. "You know what I want to do? Go to TG&Y."

Those were magic words to us. TG&Y was the dime store a few blocks away, where every so often our uncles or Vivian would take us and buy us a toy. It was where the motorcycle policemen Hugh had given us, mine forever lost in the sandbox in the park, had come from. I had once seen a bin in the toy aisle in which dozens more were displayed, all crowded together and facing the same direction, gripping their handlebars, all wearing an identical determined expression. In their multitudes, they were infinitely more purposeful than my lost policeman had seemed on his own.

Emmett washed his cereal bowl out in the sink and grabbed a shirt from the narrow closet next to the kitchen. Then we walked down the stairs and got into the car with Frank while Emmett ran into the house to tell Babi—who was the only one at home—that they were taking Danny and me to the dime store. In just a few minutes we were happily wandering the aisles of the toy department, inspecting the cap guns in their holsters, the windup metal robots, the bags of plastic cowboys and Indians, and army men on revolving racks. Since choosing one thing meant not choosing another, our deliberations were intense, and so leisurely that it was usually infuriating to the adults who trailed behind us, looking at their watches.

But today was different. Frank no longer had a job and Emmett had forsaken his, at least for the day. They were strangely unhurried and even seemed to enjoy the way that Danny or I or both of us would pick up something, determine that it was what we wanted, and get all the way to the checkout counter only to be seized by doubt and to return again to the toy aisles and their intimidating abundance of possibilities.

In the end we both chose the same thing: a rubber-band-powered airplane with a red plastic propeller and matching red plastic wheels—a much more imposing aircraft than the simple ten-cent balsa-wood gliders we were used to. My imagination was already outpacing any aerodynamics that this plane could possibly be capable of. As we got back into the car, I pictured it soaring for hours like the plane that Sky King flew on TV, and I also projected myself into its cockpit, somehow confident that as it flew I would not merely be observing from the ground but be its pilot, experiencing along with the plane the unbounded thrill of ranging across the sky.

The park behind our house was the nearest place to fly the airplanes, but Frank decided to drive us to another, bigger park close to downtown, several miles away.

"We're at large today," he said, "so let's really be at large. Let's strike out for new territory."

The leopard was also still at large, but Frank and Emmett had apparently decided that we didn't need to be bound anymore by Bethie's rule to stay inside. The citywide hunt, though, was still very much on. There were still Army helicopters above us, and pickup trucks whose beds were full of exuberant young men armed with rifles.

Frank turned on the radio as he drove. "Good leopardhunting weather today!" an announcer declared. "Everybody's out on the streets again, armed with everything from cap guns to bazookas!"

"Look at that," Emmett said, staring out the open window at a plane cruising above us at low altitude. "A B-25. What are they planning to do, drop bombs on him?"

"I'm starting to feel stupid just driving around," Frank said. "We've got the guns in the trunk, let's take the boys home and—"

"No!" Danny said. "You said you'd take us to fly our airplanes."

"That's what we're doing," Emmett told him. "Just hold your horses for a minute."

We pulled up to the park and Danny and I tumbled out of the car and ran across the grass. As we ran, we turned the plane's propellers to wind up their rubber-band engines. Frank stayed behind, sitting in the driver's seat with the motor running and listening to the radio.

I still felt exposed in an open place like this city park, but a few days of learning about the hunting practices of leopards made the fear that we would be attacked in the daytime manageable. And in an odd way the lecture we had just received an hour before from the TV big-game hunter, when he warned us to keep inside, had tamped down that fear even more. By leaving the TV screen and manifesting into the world, acting peeved and put-upon like an ordinary human, he had somehow forfeited his credibility. He had seemed small next to Frank, like somebody who was pretending to be something he was not.

My focus now was not on the leopard but on our new airplanes. They proved to be cruelly disappointing. No matter how tight we wound the rubber bands, when we released the planes they merely teetered in the air for a few yards before nose-diving into the grass, not gracefully gliding to a landing on their red wheels as I had imagined.

It was that gap between my imagination and the reality of my plane's performance that pushed me over the edge into the only full-scale childhood tantrum I can remember.

"It doesn't work!" I cried in outrage, throwing the fragile craft down onto the grass.

"Hold on now," Emmett said. He picked the plane up and straightened its wings and meticulously wound up the rubber band again, then let it loose. It flew, but it didn't soar. It just coasted a little farther than it had when I launched it and then dove just as unceremoniously into the grass.

"It's supposed to fly!" I wailed. "But it doesn't! I don't want it!"

I realized I was putting on a demonstration, but the tears were sluicing down my face all the same, a genuine explosion of frustration and confusion, the pent-up outrage a child can feel when the world doesn't conform to the template he has created in his head. Danny called me a baby. Frank had left the car and joined us by then. He did his best along with Emmett to try to talk me back into reason. But reason has no sway over a childhood outburst, and all the adults could do was stand back and shrug in disgust.

To deliberately inflame them further, I ran over to my plane, picked it up off the grass, and threw it down as hard as I could. It was sturdier than I thought—neither of its wings broke. Frustrated that my demonstration of outrage had not reached the crescendo I planned, I decided to stomp on the plane with my foot.

Frank grabbed me before I could accomplish it. He picked me up and held me tight in his arms as I wriggled in defiance to get free. I finally managed it, but by that time Emmett had picked up the plane and said he wouldn't give it back to me until I'd calmed down.

I wanted to calm down very much. By that point I was ashamed of myself and aware of how horrible I must seem to my uncles, who had gone out of their way to buy me a toy only to have to watch me violently spurn their generosity. But I was a little boy and not in control of myself, or maybe I needed to keep the drama up for a little longer so I could make a statement and be in control of myself in my own time.

"Where did this come from?" I heard Frank say as my outrage began to subside into hiccups. He was talking about something he had just picked up from the grass, something that had fallen out of my shorts pocket while he and I had been wrestling. It was the Thunderbird patch I had found in the basement.

"Grady took it," Danny said.

"I didn't take it!" I told him. "It's mine!"

"No, it's not yours, Grady." Frank's voice was so calm it verged on anger. "It's mine."

He slipped the patch into his shirt pocket.

"If you boys want to see something of mine, ask me," he said. "I'd be more than happy to show it to you. But I don't like people pawing over my stuff, okay?"

I added this rebuke to my list of grievances against the universe, but by that time it didn't much matter, since my outburst was running its course and I was calming down.

"How about this," Emmett said. "You two give your uncle Frank and me a quick turn with these airplanes. We'll show you how you can make them fly if you're just a little bit calmer when you wind them up."

"*I* was calm!" Danny said in an outraged voice. "It was Grady who was a little baby about it."

I protested angrily against that characterization of myself, though I knew it was true. If I hadn't been smaller than my brother, and naturally deferential to our birth order, I might have launched myself at him to prove that I wasn't a baby and he was a liar. But I was also out of energy. I was in a kind of post-tantrum afterglow in which I felt contentedly depleted and knew that despite my behavior, all would be forgiven.

Danny and I gave our uncles a turn at flying the airplanes and watched as the windup aircraft flew more or less the way they were supposed to when given over to the patience and finesse of adults. We jealously seized them back after one flight, and though we did slightly better than we had before, the planes still sputtered gracelessly for only a few yards and then nose-dived again into a crash landing. After another frustrating attempt, one of the wings on Danny's plane cracked on impact with the ground. Emmett picked it up and said he would fix it later with Scotch tape.

"I don't care," Danny said. He was bored by then.

"Well, you two sure have a way of looking a gift horse in the mouth," Emmett said.

"What's a gift horse?" I asked.

"A gift horse is someone who tries to do something nice for somebody and gets stabbed in the back for his efforts."

He and Frank were already walking back to the car, so we followed, feeling chastened without being all that clear about what our transgression had been and what it had to do with a horse lying dead on the ground with a knife protruding from it.

"Look at that helicopter," Frank said when we were all in the car. He had not yet turned on the ignition and was looking off in the distance over the steering wheel. "It's making these big circles like it's found something."

He started the car. The engine turned over and a moment later the radio came back on. "We are receiving scattered reports," the announcer said, "that the leopard may have been sighted once again, northeast of the city in the Witcher vicinity."

"That's about where that helicopter's circling," Emmett said to Frank.

The man on the radio went on to talk about a farmer whose cows had been stampeded and whose dogs had come home with mysterious claw marks on their bodies. Another person had reported hearing an unearthly cry in the night, and another claimed that he had seen print marks along the creek that ran behind his house.

From the back seat, I watched my uncles' faces as they exchanged assessing looks. I could tell how much they wanted to join the hunt, and I understood that the only thing keeping them from doing so was the fact that Danny and I were with them.

I'm not sure exactly what motivated me to burst out with what I said next. Maybe it had something to do with an accumulating sense of my own weakness: my fear of climbing to the next tier of the park fountain; the waking dreams of malevolent shapes and the sharply delineated nightmares of prowling beasts; the memory of myself hiding under the bed while my mother tried to coax me out. But I was also tired of who I was and who I sensed I was becoming, the boy who would never grow out of being a baby brother, who when it was time to take a chance would always hesitate, and whose hesitation would grow into paralysis. But maybe that didn't have to be me. Maybe I had a chance to be more like Big Dan, the way he had been when he had turned to that man at the drugstore counter and shut him down by saying "Hey!" Maybe even, as Bethie had confided to me as I cowered under the bed, I had something of my father in me, some slumbering trace of courage and daring, and that it was therefore possible to enlarge the definition of myself.

These could not have been actual deliberations, actual thoughts. I put them down here so many decades later only in a rhetorical attempt to understand who I might have been at that moment, and what caused me to grab the back of the bench seat in which my uncles were sitting, push myself forward until my head was between theirs, and call out in a self-consciously blustery voice that shocked everyone in the car, not least myself, "Let's go get that leopard!"

18

When they heard my declaration, Frank and Emmett laughed. But the laughter lasted only for a moment, and then the glance between them told me that they were reacting as if I had somehow given them permission.

Frank turned around and looked at me and then at Danny.

"So that's what you boys want to do? Go after that leopard?"

I said yes, though now that I saw they were serious I said so in a less excited voice than I had a moment before.

"We need guns!" Danny said.

"You don't need guns," Frank said. "*We* do. And don't worry, they're in the trunk."

"Maybe we should—" Emmett said, but Frank interrupted him before he could finish his thought.

"And you two don't tell anybody, especially your mother. Is that a deal?"

We said it was a deal.

"Now, don't get excited," Emmett told us. "All that's going

to happen, probably, is that we just keep driving around. And in the unlikely event that something does happen, you two are not going to get out of the car under any circumstances. Got that?"

We nodded in agreement, and Frank gripped the gearshift and put the car into drive. He drove east, toward the outskirts of the city, the solemn gray capitol building receding into the distance on our left. There were a lot of other cars and trucks cruising in the same general direction, all of them on the hunt for the leopard, but at every opportunity Frank got off the main streets and drove down roads that were increasingly less trafficked, and so narrow that the thick foliage on either side almost met above us in midair.

It was on one of those roads on the fringes of the city that we encountered a cluster of jeeps and trucks forming a roadblock. National Guard troops were disembarking from the back of one of the canvas-sided trucks. They wore billed fatigue caps and carried rifles. Several of the soldiers studied a map laid out on the hood of a jeep, and another stood in the middle of the road speaking to someone over a walkie-talkie.

One of the men approached our car when it stopped at the roadblock. Frank set his elbow on the open window and leaned out to speak to him.

"Something happening?" he asked.

The soldier who answered him looked intimidatingly powerful to me, though I have a clear memory of the pimples on his pale, sunburnt face, so I doubt he was over eighteen. He said that we would have to turn around.

"Why is that?" Frank asked him.

"Because there's some activity up ahead."

"Leopard activity?"

"Can't say, sir."

"How's the 45th doing these days? Got a lot of guys in Korea?"

"Quite a few, yessir. But you'll have to—"

Frank reached into his shirt pocket and held out the patch with the yellow bird he had just confiscated from me. He displayed it like a policeman displaying his badge.

"My brother here's a T-patcher, but I'm a Thunderbird like you guys. 'Semper Anticus,' right?"

"Sir?"

"The motto—'Always Forward.' They still teach you that?"

"Oh, yeah."

"Like when you were still in grade school, and some of us were going forward into Germany."

The soldier suddenly seemed a lot younger as he stood there trying to process what Frank was telling him.

"So," Frank said, "we'd like to go forward."

"I can't let you do that."

Frank sat there tapping the steering wheel and sort of whistling, like he was deliberating what to say next. I could only see the back of his head, but there must have been some tension in his face, because I heard Emmett say, "Let it go, Frank."

By that time another man was headed our way—he looked older and surer of himself. He leaned down to the window and asked if there was any trouble.

"No trouble, Sergeant," Frank told him. "I was just telling the general here that I've got my M1 in the trunk and I'd be as happy to shoot a leopard with it as I was shooting Krauts. Thought you guys might appreciate the help."

"We don't need any help." The sergeant's voice was cold.

"Listen, I was with the 157th over in—"

"I don't care where you were. Turn this car around and get out of here."

"All right," Frank said after another silence. "I will if you get out of my fucking way."

The sergeant and the private backed up, and Frank made a violent U-turn that clipped the weeds along the side of the road and sent us back in the other direction with a tire-squealing, fishtailing salute.

He looked back over his shoulder at Danny and me and smiled. "Pardon my language, gentlemen, but that guy had it coming."

"Slow down!" Emmett said. "We've got kids in the car."

"You're right." Frank eased off on the accelerator and we were at cruising speed again, driving down a country road. I didn't know how to make sense of the altercation we had just witnessed, but things seemed all right now, with Frank doing his best to settle his temper.

"I wonder who decided the National Guard was qualified to be big-game hunters anyway," he said to Emmett.

"Probably the same people who decided we were."

"That's how you're treated," he called back to us, "when you volunteer to fight for your country. Remember that."

"Stop talking to them like that, Frank," Emmett said. "They don't need to hear stuff like that."

Frank stopped talking, but I noticed the tight grip he had on the steering wheel, and even a confused boy could detect the bitterness he was struggling to beat back before it overwhelmed him.

It would be many years later, and too late to make any difference, that I began to wonder what might have helped forge that bitterness. It wasn't until I was in my fifties, more than twice the age Frank had been when he fought in the war, that my curiosity led me to make a few phone calls and enter a few terms in one of those now-forgotten search engines in the early days of the Internet. I discovered that his military records, along with those of millions of other veterans, had been destroyed in a catastrophic 1973 fire that swept through the National Personnel Records Center in St. Louis. That was enough of a roadblock, during a busy time of my life when General Motors had issued a recall on several of its models and the dealership was having trouble keeping up with the work, to sidetrack me for another few years.

Then one day I was having lunch with a customer, a retired colonel who had bought a half-dozen cars from me over the years, with whom I had become friendly and who was a regular at my book club. He was something of a historian, who had written several privately published accounts of various regiments and the engagements they had fought in. Out of the blue, remembering that patch I had found in the basement, the one that Frank had shown to that National Guard soldier like a credential, I asked him what he knew about the Thunderbirds of the 45th Division. It ended up being a long lunch, as he recounted the history of the 45th from their landing at Sicily until their march into Munich at the end of the war two years later. He recommended some books to read, and I told him the few details I had managed to pick up about Frank's service history.

When we met again, I had read the books and he had done his own research and made some calls to military historians and even to some surviving members of Frank's regiment, the 157th. What I took away from those books was the sheer improbability of any one soldier surviving the amount of combat Frank must have seen, hundreds of days of unrelenting fighting throughout Italy and France and Germany, vicious battles in the forests of the Vosges Mountains, or along the Siegfried Line, or against heavily fortified cities like Aschaffenburg and Nuremberg. He would have seen many, if not most, of his friends killed or severely wounded as German machine-gun fire tore into them from hidden places in the dense forest undergrowth, or as they were blown apart by mines, or as enemy shells exploded in the trees above them and shredded their bodies with a penetrating rain of shrapnel and wood splinters. Frank's nerves would have been stretched so tight, for so long, that it would have been impossible for him to ever completely settle back into something like mere wariness.

And all that was before they got to Dachau. They had no idea what they were walking toward as they marched down the railroad tracks into what they thought was some sort of POW camp or German military complex on the edge of the city. There was an unholy stench arising from the thirty-nine boxcars of a stopped train. Stacked inside the boxcars were two thousand emaciated corpses. As the men advanced into the camp, they came upon more bodies, piled up outside barracks and other buildings near the crematorium, left to rot instead of being incinerated, because the Germans had run out of coal to fire the ovens. But over thirty thousand people were still alive, so many of them wasted away by starvation that it was hard for their liberators to tell if the skeletal forms they encountered still had any life in them. The Thunderbirds wept in bewilderment and rage.

My friend the colonel had been able to determine that Frank had been a member of I Company, but that was where his research trail ended. It would probably be impossible to find out, he said, whether my uncle had been one of the men who had lined a group of German soldiers who had surrendered up against a wall at the edge of a coal yard. Their prisoners were Waffen-SS, elite fighters who were quartered at the adjacent garrison but not members of the SS-Totenkopfverbände, the guard unit that actually ran the camp and committed the atrocities the Americans had seen. That mattered little to the Thunderbirds of I Company, or at least to the soldiers who mowed the prisoners down with machine-gun and rifle fire.

My friend, as we sat there eating lunch, was unforgiving of that incident. He had spent his career in the Army, and his own personal honor was based on a creed of discipline. What happened that day in the Dachau coal yard, he said, had been—pure and simple—a war crime. I believed that too, from the comfort of my booth in Applebee's. But in truth I wondered whether, if I had experienced a fraction of what Frank had, even my own naturally mild disposition or any code of conduct would have spared me from picking up my rifle and firing at those men with their hands in the air.

I'll never have to know if Frank had been one of those soldiers who fired upon the German prisoners. Having learned what he went through before he got to Dachau, and having witnessed as a child his mysterious simmering grievances, I can't honestly rule it out. But he was also Big Dan's son, and when he was growing up he must have experienced moments like the one I had at that drugstore counter, when my grandfather shut down with a single word the man who had been terrorizing that young Black girl—a moment that created a working template for me of how a man should behave. So I can also imagine another scenario for Frank at Dachau, and that's the version I choose to believe. The young man who was still imprinted with those lessons from his father—the Frank I had seen in church kneeling at the pew with his eyes shut tight, doing his honest best to pray—would have done something to try to stop the slaughter, or at least turned away in horror and ordered the surviving men under his command not to participate.

I remember watching Frank's face in the rearview mirror as he drove through the outskirts of Oklahoma City searching for the leopard. I suspect that the vigilance I saw in his eyes— his hunter's eyes—was something that had developed during the war and that he was deploying now like an athlete slipping back into a sport for which he had an exquisite muscle memory. As he scanned the roadside from the passenger-side window, Emmett had much the same look. For all the tension in their faces, maybe they were relaxed in spirit to be back in a world that made visceral sense to them. Not the world of a Chevrolet dealership or an anonymous drafting table, a world where they lived next door to their parents and still under their chastening scrutiny, but one in which skills that had once crucially mattered were now suddenly relevant again.

Frank took every turn he came to, leading us deeper into a maze of often unpaved rural roads passing through sparsely populated settlements with dilapidated houses. The houses had no lawns, just broad expanses of weedy ground or red dirt where children our age sat in the branches of trees or on tire swings watching us pass. The deeper we drove into this warren of semiresidential streets, the fewer cars we encountered. Most of the leopard hunters had stuck to the main roads, following questionable leads on the radio about sightings, or trailing some Army jeep or other promising vehicle whose occupants somehow gave the impression that they were on to something. The helicopter whose circling pattern had led us to this part of the city was no longer in the sky, having either moved on to scout out another quadrant or gone back for refueling.

Emmett looked at his watch and turned to Frank. "It's almost five o'clock. Maybe we ought to get the boys home before Bethie gets off work."

Frank slowly nodded his head but kept driving. He glanced at Danny and me through the rearview mirror. "Remember, you don't tell your mother or anybody else what we've been up to."

"Can we tell her we went to the dime store?" I asked. "And to the park?"

"Absolutely," Emmett said. "Tell her that. And it's true."

I was relieved. It meant I would not have to bear the frightening responsibility of a total lie.

"We don't want to upset your mother," Emmett went on. "She's got plenty to deal with as it is. It's not easy being the mother to two young boys, did you know that?"

We said yes, we knew that, but we didn't really. We had seen Bethie, after a long shift at the hospital, standing over the stove in our little apartment, making our supper as Danny and I nagged her unmercifully about going out to play or watching TV, or as we threw ourselves into a fight, with Danny holding me down on the floor and me screaming in piteous outrage. But we were children, unconcerned about how or whether our behavior had anything to do with the fact that she stood there with stoic tears streaming down her face as she fried the baloney for our sandwiches.

"I'll tell you what, though," Frank said, looking at us through the rearview mirror again. "Your father would have been right out here with us."

"You're right," Emmett agreed. "I wish Burt had lived to see this. He would have loved nothing better than to go on an Oklahoma leopard safari with his two boys and his two crazy brothers-in-law."

Emmett shifted in his seat and looked back at us, smiling. He seemed to have forgotten all about staring out the window for a glimpse of the escaped leopard. He told us about the first time they had seen our father. The war had ended, he said, everyone was back and living at home, Frank and Emmett and Bethie all discharged from the Army, Vivian in business school.

"So one day your mother says, 'Oh, by the way, we might have a visitor.' She'd been telling us about this pilot she'd met at the base in Ephrata and had a few dates with. She acted like it was no big deal. Your mother happened to be the best-looking nurse in the Army, in case you didn't know. She was in demand, never had a night off without a couple of captains getting into an argument about who got to take her out."

Emmett went on to tell us about how Burt had been assigned after the war to the recruiting office in Omaha, and flew himself down to Oklahoma City one weekend in an Army Air Forces two-engine trainer.

"He pulled up to the curb in front of the house in a cab and stepped out in his uniform with this big grin on his face and his hand out. 'You must be Frank, you must be Emmett, why who else could this be but the one and only Vivian! Mr. and Mrs. Brennan, it's a real honor to meet you both, blah blah

blah.' He already knew everything about everybody in the family. And boy, you should have seen the way he looked at your mother standing there on the lawn!

"We knew right away that she'd already made up her mind to marry him. I think she kept it a secret just because she wanted everybody to sort of get the full dose all at once. She was pretty sure none of us was going to say he wasn't good enough for our sister. He had—what would you say, Frank?"

"Confidence."

" 'Confidence' is as good a word as any. That's what it takes to be a fighter pilot and not just a dogface like your two uncles up here."

They went on for a few more minutes, talking about this mysterious man who was far less real to Danny and me than they were, but who had such a looming command over the direction of all our lives.

"That day he came to visit," Frank said, "we must have stayed up with him till past midnight, talking about the war, talking about—"

He broke off, suddenly silent and alert. Up ahead a car had stopped on the side of the road. And a woman was running toward us, waving us down and yelling that she had just seen the leopard.

19

"Stay here," Frank barked at Danny and me as he and Emmett jumped out of the car and went to talk to the woman.

We vaulted over into the front seat so we could get a better view of what was happening. The woman was middle-aged, her hair in curlers beneath a scarf. She was talking energetically to our uncles, gesturing toward the barely perceptible seam of a creek bed that ran from the culvert beneath the road through the thick, stunted woods.

The woman was clearly excited, but she had a soft voice and even though the windows of the car were rolled down we couldn't make out much of what she was saying, except that her husband had just run off in pursuit of the leopard.

"He didn't even have a gun!" she said.

Frank and Emmett talked to her a moment more; then Frank walked back to our car with his keys in his hand.

"Let's roll those windows up," he told us, then he went to the back of the car and was in the process of opening the trunk when the woman's husband reappeared. Frank closed the trunk without taking out his rifle and jogged back to where the man was now standing. We had cranked up the windows when Frank demanded that we do so, so we couldn't hear what everybody was saying. The man wore a sweat-soaked peach-colored shirt. Perspiration streamed down his face from the brim of his hat. He had a cigar in his mouth and was gnawing on it as Emmett pulled a city map out of his pocket and they all stood studying it in the middle of the road. After a few minutes the man and the woman got back in their car and drove away. Frank and Emmett came back and opened the doors to the front seat and scooted us into the back.

"Going off into that brush after a leopard without a rifle," Frank said to Emmett. "Takes all kinds."

"Did he find the leopard?" I asked.

"He thinks so," Emmett said. "He says he saw something moving in the trees, him and his wife both. Crazy guy just got out of the car and started running after it. I don't know what he was expecting to do if he caught up to it."

"So what are *we* doing?" Danny asked.

"Oh, we're just going to drive around a little while," Frank said. "Then get you two home for dinner."

He drove slowly ahead, pulling off onto yet another side road after about a mile. I wasn't sure whether at this point I was deflated or relieved. The boldness I had felt at the beginning of this expedition was ebbing away as the prospect of actually encountering a leopard began to seem real. But Danny was indignant—he didn't want to go home and eat dinner, he wanted to find the leopard. And because his indignation gave me courage, I shouted that I didn't want to give up, either.

"Settle down," Frank told us. "We're on thin ice with your mother as it is, and—"

"There he is!" Danny suddenly screeched. "I saw him! I saw him!"

"No you didn't," Emmett said, "you just—"

"I did! Stop the car! I saw him!"

Frank shrugged and pulled the car to a stop along the grassy shoulder of a road that was barely wider than the car we were in.

"Where did you see it, Danny?"

"Back there!"

He stabbed his finger at the glass of the rear window.

"Okay, you two stay here."

Frank and Emmett got out and walked around to the rear of the car and stood there looking for a long time with their hands in their pockets. We watched them through the rear window, wondering if they were seeing anything, what they were saying to each other. We had stopped at a place so lonely and scraggly it seemed threatening. I know now from studying old maps that we weren't more than two or three miles beyond the familiar eastern margins of Oklahoma City. But in those days, before endless urban sprawl, leaving the outer edges of a city was as abrupt an experience as falling off a cliff. We were in what we called back then "the country." A thick forest of black-jack oak crowded in on the road from either side. There were no other cars and no buildings visible, just a deeply shaded and rutty dirt road that amounted to a long driveway leading to no house that I could see, though there was a rusting mailbox a few yards away from where we were parked.

"Did you really see the leopard?" I asked Danny.

"Shut up!" he said. His eyes were fixed on the dark tangle of vegetation, his tongue protruding in concentration.

Frank and Emmett were just then turning to get back into the car when Danny screamed again.

"There!"

And we all saw—something. Or maybe I was just reacting to the fact that everybody else had seen something, and the need to see it myself was so powerful that the leopard just appeared in my mind. Children are primed for hallucinatory manifestations of the invisible workings of their imaginations. It had happened to me the week before, when I had seen a malicious beast lingering in the hallway, ready to pounce on me if I tried to make it to the safety of my mother's bedroom.

Today my mind conjured up, or my eyes actually saw, a flash of yellowish fur in the undergrowth of that stunted roadside forest. Danny excitedly cranked down the back seat window and yelled at our uncles.

"Did you see it?"

"Calm down, Danny," Frank said. "Yeah, we saw something."

"We can't just leave the boys here on the side of the road," we heard Emmett tell Frank.

Frank nodded his head as he peered into the vegetation for another glimpse of the animal. Then he said to his brother, "I'll stay with them. You go."

Emmett looked at him in mild surprise. "You sure?"

"Sure, maybe you'll flush him out and I'll get a shot at him from right here anyway."

They opened the trunk and took out their rifles. Emmett's was a deer rifle I had seen in a cabinet in their apartment. I had never known either of my uncles to go hunting, so I suspect the rifle wasn't originally Emmett's but a hand-me-down from Big Dan, who had probably used it when he was growing up on the family farm in Kansas. Frank retrieved the M1 he had managed to hold on to after the war. It was heavier than Emmett's deer rifle, with a deep wooden stock. We watched, fascinated, as he loaded a clip into it with casual mastery. The bullets were long and lethally pointed. The way they were crowded together in the clip reminded me of Crayolas in a brand-new box, though there was nothing colorful about them, unless you counted the copper sheen brought out by the late-afternoon sun.

From the rear window we saw Emmett start off. He did so without ceremony or any parting words, just walked into the blackjack thicket, holding his rifle in one hand as he used the other to push away branches or vines. He wore a white shirt and khaki pants. For a while we caught glimpses of fabric through the intergrown vegetation, and then—as if he had entered a tunnel—we saw no more of him.

"Do you think he's going to find it?" Danny asked.

"I don't know," Frank said. He was standing at the side of the car, smoking a cigarette, holding his heavy rifle with the sling dangling. "Let's be quiet for now, okay? We don't want the leopard to know we're here."

"So it's really the leopard?" I asked.

"Might be. Might not be. But let's be quiet so we can have a chance to find out."

We obeyed and were quiet, sitting in the back seat of the car in the summer heat. I could see the sweat on Frank's face as he bent down to grind out his cigarette under his foot. I could see the muscular tension in his forearm as he held the rifle. I felt oddly safe. Even though our window was now open, Frank was standing in front of it, and I knew as clearly as I knew anything that he would continue standing in front of it if the leopard suddenly leapt out of the brush and tried to reach his nephews. I had the sense that I was experiencing in this moment what my brother felt when he was maneuvering park benches to climb up to the top of that water fountain in the park: not fear, but excitement. I wondered: had I suddenly grown older, was I now less of a child than I had been only a few days before?

We sat there for maybe fifteen minutes, forcing ourselves into uncharacteristic stillness and silence. I kept staring at the dark forest that had swallowed Emmett up, wondering how he could ever find his way back. The longer it took for anything to happen, the more the balance between excitement and fear began to shift back to where it had been before. I looked at Danny for reassurance, but his focus was so intense and expectant that I couldn't get him to notice me. I tugged at his arm, but he shook it away from my grasp and kept staring ahead as if he had just swatted a mosquito whose presence he had barely felt.

Then we heard a sound in the distance, a sound like the slap of a screen door. The only rifle shots I had ever heard were on TV, ricocheting off the boulders that cowboy heroes like the Lone Ranger or Hopalong Cassidy took cover behind. This was different, and I'm not sure I would have recognized it as gunfire if Frank's body had not immediately seized up as he gripped his Army rifle with both hands.

"What was that?" Danny and I both asked him at once.

"Nothing."

"Did he shoot the leopard?"

"I'll let you know when I find out myself."

I knew that Frank desperately wanted to run into the woods

himself and join the hunt. I could tell he was thinking about it by the way he kept looking off into the distance and then back at us in the car. But he stood firm where he was, as tense as a coiled snake, waiting to hear what had just happened.

Then we heard Emmett yelling "Start the car! Start the car!" He was coming up the long dirt driveway holding his rifle in front of him and running faster than I had ever seen him—or anyone else—run before.

We heard Frank mutter to himself—"What the hell?"—but he didn't ask any questions or waste any movement. He threw his rifle back into the trunk, ran around to the driver's-side door, and started the engine just as Emmett leapt into the passenger seat and yelled, "Go! Go! Go!"

20

Frank didn't ask what had happened at first. He just drove. It was left to Danny and me to ask excitable questions from the back seat that neither of our uncles had time to pay any attention to. I could see Frank's eyes in the rearview mirror, focused as sharply as a hawk's on the road behind us. Emmett had turned halfway around and was tapping his hand nervously on the upholstered seat as he too stared into the distance.

"How come we're running away?" I finally asked.

"Don't worry about it," Emmett said. "Everything's okay."

He turned to Frank. "You see that truck?"

"Yeah, I see it," Frank said, without shifting his eyes from the rearview mirror. "There's another car behind it too."

"Shit."

"Better tell me what's going on."

Emmett glanced back at us, then leaned closer to Frank and covered his mouth as he spoke.

"Christ almighty!" Frank said.

"We can't hear!" Danny said.

"That's all right, you don't need to hear anything right now."

Frank made a hard left turn off the narrow rural road onto something that resembled a normal city street. The momentum caused Danny and me to tumble from one side of the car to the other in the back seat.

"Slow down!" Emmett said. "We've got kids in the car."

"Yeah, but in case you haven't noticed we've also got somebody on our tail who's not too happy with us."

While they were talking, the car that had appeared behind the truck swung out into the left lane and came scorching past us on a straightaway at what must have been over ninety miles per hour. Frank mashed down on the accelerator when he saw it happening, but I suppose in order not to risk our lives he eased up and let the car pass. It was an old Ford sedan that had once been blue but had faded to the color of a pallid sky, almost the color of the gray primer paint on its fenders. But judging by the speed it was capable of, somebody had been paying loving attention to its motor.

There were two people in the car, both Black men, both young—probably teenagers, sixteen or seventeen years old. But they looked very angry and very dangerous.

Frank made another sharp turn, and suddenly we were in a place that I recognized. It was the parking lot of Springlake, the amusement park a few miles from the zoo. We had always approached Springlake from a different entrance on another street, and to see it unexpectedly pop into view, and from a different angle, was disorienting, especially since just moments before I thought we had been beyond the edge of the world. The frantic circumstances that had brought us here were also bewildering, and neither Frank nor Emmett seemed willing to explain them.

"Oh, fuck!" Emmett said. The car that had raced ahead of us had been out of sight for a few minutes, but now it cut in front of us so sharply that Frank had to smash on the brakes, sending Danny and me bumping against the front seat. We were now stopped between a row of parked cars, and there was no way to get around the roadblock that had appeared in front—and behind us the truck that had been following us now nosed up to our rear bumper.

Frank's rifle was in the trunk, but he reached over to grab the deer rifle that Emmett was still holding.

"No!" Emmett said, jerking it away. "Are you crazy? You want to start a gunfight with the boys in the car?"

Frank muttered something I didn't hear, then opened the door and walked ahead to meet the two men who had cut us off and had now leaped out of their own car. Frank was taller than they were, and older. But neither of those advantages seemed to make a difference at a moment when the men were boiling over with rage.

Emmett turned to Danny and me. "Do you promise me you'll stay in the car? Promise?"

We said we would. What was happening around us was too enormously intimidating for even Danny to want to be a part of it.

Emmett laid his rifle across the floorboard in front of him. "Do not touch that!" he commanded. Then he got out of the car and went to join the confrontation.

The two young Black men were yelling at Frank and Emmett. One of them had tears in his eyes. They spoke so rapidly, talking over each other, that I had trouble making out everything they were saying, but some of the words I caught were: "What gave you the right to do that, man? What gave you the right to do that to somebody who wasn't causing you no trouble at all?"

Neither Frank nor Emmett could have gotten a word in, but they were both gesturing for calm.

"He's the one who did it!" one of the young men said, pointing to Emmett. He was speaking to someone else now, an older man who was just now emerging from the truck that had come up behind us. The man glanced into the window as he passed our car. He was in his fifties, wearing dungarees, an unbuttoned sport shirt over a T-shirt, and a black straw fedora that was shiny with lacquer in the sun. He shook his head when he saw us, in disapproval or even disgust that two boys had been dragged into this altercation. He gave us a half-wave and walked over to join the two young men, who I assumed were his sons, as they continued to confront Frank and Emmett.

He told them to calm down and they obeyed, fidgeting with silent anger. This man too was enraged, but his voice was level, and without all the overlapping clamor we could hear clearly what he said.

"Why would you want to shoot our dog?"

Danny and I turned to each other. I still remember the expression on my brother's face, a face that rarely registered surprise or concern but which now was wide-eyed with astonishment. Emmett hadn't shot the leopard; he had shot a dog. A dog whose yellowish fur had been visible in quick flashes through the dense tangle of undergrowth, with the dappled light from the leaves above making spotlike patterns as he moved.

"Would you like to see him?" the older man asked our

uncles—not asked, but righteously demanded. "Would you like to see what you did to our dog? He's lying back there in the dirt. I'll take you to see him!"

"I'm sorry," Emmett told him. "I'm really sorry."

"No, I want you to take a look! These boys here grew up with that dog. Want to know what his name is? Never mind—I don't care if you want to know, I'm going to tell you! It's Buster. You got a dog, your boys in there got a dog?"

"Look—" Frank said.

"Don't you 'look' me, you son of a bitch. White man thinks he can come into my neighborhood and shoot my dog!"

"I thought it was the leopard," Emmett pleaded.

At this the man turned from Frank to regard Emmett with amazement, and then with pity, and then he broke into an enraged laugh.

"The leopard! God almighty, son, are you that stupid?"

"Don't call my brother stupid!" Frank spat the words out.

By now the growing ruckus had attracted a small crowd, mostly young men and women who had been riding the rides in the park or swimming in its big pool with its towering water-slide. Some of them were still in their bathing suits. I could hear in the background the ratchety rumble of Springlake's roller coaster, the screams of the people riding it, the calls of "Marco!" and "Polo!" from the swimming pool on the other side of the fence.

And now, behind us, two more cars pulled up, and several more young Black men got out and stood there in vigilant still-ness, trying to assess what was going on. One of them held a tire iron.

"You okay, Uncle Melvin?"

The man he was addressing dismissed the question with a

wave of his hand, but he was still staring at Frank, still tense. He was a quarter-century older than Frank, but he was clearly ready to fight.

"What do you want?" Frank said to Uncle Melvin. "He already said he was sorry."

"I ain't heard *you* say you was sorry yet."

"Maybe you won't ever."

Emmett stepped in between them before they could attack each other. He reached into his back pocket for his wallet.

"Here," he said. "I made a mistake and I'm willing to pay you for all the trouble I caused. How much do you think—"

But before he could even open his wallet the older of Uncle Melvin's two sons stepped forward, grabbed the wallet, and threw it on the ground.

"You think this is about money, you—"

I saw Frank's arm flash upward with an unexpected velocity, like the spring-loaded grasshopper that hopped onto the pages of my children's book. It would have been a powerful punch if his target had been slower, but the young man saw it building and moved his head just quickly enough for Frank's fist to land glancingly on the side of his face.

"He hit him!" Danny yelled in my ear.

It was a misapplied punch, but it was enough to turn the encounter from an agitated verbal argument to an outright melee. Uncle Melvin called for calm—he knew well enough the consequences of allowing himself to get into a fight with white men. But nobody was listening to him. His nephews and his sons rushed forward as the white onlookers did the same. Danny and I watched in stupefaction from what I hoped was the safety of our car. I remember calling out "Bethie!" over and over again, and even Danny was really scared now as he saw our uncles in the middle of the fracas with their arms flailing and their shirts half torn-off. Part of my terror must have come from the understanding that they were in the wrong, that *we* were in the wrong. And yet, as I looked down at the deer rifle on the floorboard of the car, the thought passed through my mind that maybe I should grab it, that I should be ready to do anything to protect my uncles, just as I knew they would protect me if I were the one who had shot somebody's dog. But I didn't know how to shoot a rifle, so all I could do was grab my brother around the waist and cling to him and listen to myself keep calling out my mother's name.

21

The private confrontation between my uncles and the family whose dog Emmett had killed had become a fracas that quickly expanded into a full-scale riot, one that spilled over from the Springlake parking lot into the amusement park itself. I'm not sure how the word spread so fast, but carloads of angry Black people had suddenly appeared, as did a stream of white reinforcements from inside the park, young men in bathing suits with clenched fists eager to join the fight.

Springlake was segregated and had always been. Unlike the zoo, and the museum we had visited the day before, it was a private business and didn't feature a day of the week during which Black families were welcomed, or at least tolerated. With its roller coaster cresting into view all day over the fence surrounding it, with its blaring carnival music and the delighted screams emanating from its various rides, it must have been a constant taunt to the nearby citizens who were forever forbidden from entering.

From the car window, we watched as one of the Black men who had just driven up detached himself from the growing nucleus of the fight, called to several of his friends, and ran with them to the side entrance of the park, jumping over the turnstiles. The police had already arrived by then, charging into the disturbance, swinging their nightsticks at any Black head they could find. But they soon saw that there was a greater threat to peace and order than this localized fistfight— that the real battle was now inside the park, whose segregated precincts had just been breached.

I'm relating this bird's-eye account of the confrontation not so much from memory as from old newspaper articles I found online. All I saw, from the car in which we had been marooned, was the turmoil in front of us, in which about a dozen people were still involved. There was a period of time when we lost sight of Frank and Emmett and I kept turning to Danny, hoping to see in his face some sort of reassurance, or some sort of plan for what he intended for us to do. But Danny too was out of his depth. He was a little boy, just like I was, left alone with no understanding and no instructions.

The action in front of us shifted enough for a gap to open up through which I could see Frank and Emmett, their faces bloody, their clothes torn. One of the young adults who had blocked our car in the parking lot took a swing at Emmett and connected, and Emmett staggered to his knees. That's when something seized me. It was only a child-sized portion of the rage that was animating all of the participants in the fight, but it was enough to fill every cell in my body with an inchoate hunger for revenge, and to send me out of the car and into the midst of all that wildness. With windmilling arms, I tried to land punches at the people who were beating up Frank and

Emmett. I didn't care that what they had done was wrong, I didn't care that I was partly responsible; all that mattered was that these people stop hurting my uncles.

The fighting began to die away as soon as the adults noticed me and felt my tiny fists flailing away at their legs. All the Black people began to call out to each other and to back off, except for one. The man named Uncle Melvin grabbed each of my arms just above the wrists and held them tight as he got down on one knee so that his face was level to mine. I didn't know what to make of the expression in his eyes. It wasn't the look of an enemy; it was the look of an old man who just seemed to want me to understand something that he knew I probably couldn't.

"Come on now, son," he said in a pleading voice, "nobody wants you to get hurt here. This fight ain't got nothing to do with you."

He was about to say something else when a policeman's nightstick came out of nowhere and cracked into his head. He pitched over onto his side, still conscious, but dazed. By that time Frank had grabbed me from behind and was pulling me away. Several more police cars had just arrived on the scene, and the officers immediately began beating and dragging and handcuffing the Black participants in the fight without asking any questions about who had started it or what it was about.

An officer pulled Uncle Melvin unsteadily to his feet, cuffed his hands behind his back, and led him off to a patrol car. Blood was pouring down the side of his head and an unnaturally huge knot was already forming there.

Nobody arrested our uncles, but one of the policemen ordered us all back to Frank's car and told us to get inside. He looked seriously displeased with our uncles. Frank's shirt was gone, and his white undershirt was streaked with blood. One of the front pockets of Emmett's pants had been almost ripped off, so that I could see, through the dangling fabric, a glimpse of his underwear and the hairs on his bare leg.

"Jesus Christ," the policeman said to them, gesturing toward Danny and me. "You get into a fight like this in front of your kids?"

He stood outside the driver's-side window, leaning down, asking questions in an impatient voice. His face was big and he had worked up a sweat struggling with the crowd, so that fat droplets of perspiration dripped one after another from his face onto the asphalt. He wore a blue shirt and a dark-blue cap like that of the plastic motorcycle policeman I had lost in the sandbox.

"So what in the world happened here?" he began. I remember sensing even then that he regarded the white combatants as the only people he needed to interview, the only ones whose perspective counted. As far as I could tell Frank and Emmett were candid with him. They told him about coming across the couple who thought they had seen the leopard, then thinking they had seen it themselves.

"I had no intention of shooting anybody's dog," Emmett said. "That's the last thing I wanted to do."

"He tried to pay him for it," Frank said. "None of them would listen to reason. They just wanted a fight."

"Well, they sure got one," the officer said. "They got a whole riot."

I saw the police car driving away with Uncle Melvin handcuffed in the back, the second time in two days I had witnessed a Black man being taken to jail. He looked at me as he passed, or maybe he just looked in my direction. I thought how odd it was that he was still wearing his hat, after all the frantic punching and shoving that he had been a part of. It haunts me still that in that moment I don't remember feeling pity for him for losing his dog, or concern that he was being driven to jail when my uncles weren't. But I was aware, in a way I couldn't identify or quantify, that something was wrong, and that my child's ignorance about precisely what was wrong did not make me innocent.

"I'll tell you one thing," the officer said to Frank and Emmett. "A riot was the last thing we needed this week. Hard enough to keep the peace with that goddamn leopard on the loose and the whole city running around with guns. People like the two of you aren't making our work any easier."

"Sorry about that," Frank said. He wasn't looking at the officer, but out the windshield, over the top of the steering wheel. He spoke with a barely concealed tone of contempt.

"'Sorry about that,' the man says. That how you teach your sons here to speak to an officer of the law? You want me to run you in too?" He gestured toward the departing police car.

"No," Frank said in the same steely tone.

"I didn't think so."

"And they're our nephews, not our sons."

He looked at us in the back seat. "You two boys," he said, "don't you grow up to be like your uncles, you hear me?"

"Hey, now," Frank told him. "That's enough."

"I'll say when it's enough."

I could see the tension in Frank's shoulders and the color rising in his face. In the passenger seat, Emmett said nothing. He had been sitting there without speaking or responding ever since he had told the officer about shooting the dog. Now it seemed he just wanted to be alone.

"Well, I'm waiting," Frank told the officer.

"For what?"

"For you to stop jawing and let us—"

"All right, if that's the way you want this to go, maybe you better just get out of the car right now. I hate to arrest you in front of these children but by God I just might."

Frank pushed open the door and leapt out of the car and stood up right in front of the Oklahoma City policeman, staring him in the face.

"You just might, huh?"

The officer got out his handcuffs and told him to turn around, and that's when Frank punched him in the stomach. In an instant, two more policemen appeared, and as they approached Frank just smiled and put his hands out in front of him for the handcuffs. They arrested Emmett too.

"You can't just leave our nephews here by themselves," Emmett told the police as he was handcuffed. "Let us at least call their—"

That's when I saw my mother running to us. It was early evening by then, late in a summer day, and the white nurse's uniform she wore was blazingly vivid. Without a thought, I pulled up on the door handle of the back seat, opened the door, and raced to meet her. At that moment, I thought she really had heard me calling her name, that my voice had somehow carried all the way to her across Oklahoma City. It still seems somehow magical that she appeared at the right moment, in the right place, to grab me in her arms.

She would remain a very religious woman all her long life, someone who believed that intuition was a whispered spiritual message from God, or the Virgin Mary, or the guardian angels she still believed, up until her death, watched over her and everyone she loved. But there had also been plenty of earthly evidence that day to put her on the alert. She had come home from work to find that her children were still out with Frank and Emmett, and an hour later they had not yet come home. Then she had heard on the radio a live report about the riot that was taking place in Springlake, and her already anxious mind leapt to the not-quite-logical but insistent conclusion that we were somehow involved.

Hugh had showed up at the house at about that same time. They had planned to go out for dinner, but in her concern Bethie had forgotten all about that, had not even changed out of her uniform. He had volunteered at once to drive her to Springlake, and that was why I saw her running toward us from Hugh's blue Oldsmobile 88.

Hugh waited discreetly in the background as she gathered me and Danny to her and stared in tearful bewilderment as her two brothers were led in handcuffs across the parking lot.

"Are the boys okay?" Frank called back to her. His voice sounded oddly plaintive, no more bravado or contempt in it. Emmett kept staring straight ahead, afraid to look at his sister. Bethie nodded without saying anything, then confirmed to a police officer that we were her children and she was taking us home. It was left to us to tell her what had happened. She listened to our rushed story of Emmett accidentally shooting the dog and the subsequent showdown with its owners here on the edge of Springlake. The riot that it had sparked was not yet fully suppressed, judging by the dozen or so police cars that were still in the park, and the cordons of police officers guarding the entrances. To my surprise, she didn't appear angry; she was still cushioned by the relief of finding her sons alive and unhurt. But the disappointment visible in her face as she watched her brothers being led away, with their bruises and cuts and torn shirts and pants, was crushing. If she ever looked at me like that, I decided, I wouldn't be able to live.

Hugh remained behind at the car, careful not to insert himself into such an intricate family drama. As Bethie led us back in his direction, he greeted us with a calm hello and opened the back door to his big car.

As we drove off, I stared back through the rear window at Frank and Emmett as they were ushered roughly into the back seat of a police car that would take them to jail. I felt that we were all abandoning them, leaving them alone in their humiliation.

Something erupted from me then. Partly it must have been a release of the fear that I had been experiencing for the last few hours but which—with one frightening, incomprehensible moment following after the next—my body had not been able to relax itself enough to express.

I let out a sound I had never heard myself or Danny or anyone else make. It was a wail, a caterwauling scream that I could not control or even associate with my own voice. But when I looked at Danny, the wild, uncomprehending expression on his face confirmed that the sound was coming from me. I've wondered for many years what caused this particular outburst. I certainly didn't know at the time. It must have had something to do with being in a near-stranger's car, watching as my handcuffed uncles grew smaller and smaller in the distance, these two men who were the fathers I had known and who I now feared would no longer be allowed to fill that role. My mother's withering, pitying look had stripped something essential from them, and made plain to me, in a way I couldn't tolerate knowing, that they too were susceptible to being powerless and forlorn.

22

"Please stop the car," I heard Bethie tell Hugh, though her voice was barely audible to me over the sound of my own screaming.

We were heading toward home on Eastern, a street whose name was changed long ago to Martin Luther King Avenue. Hugh pulled onto a side street that led to the old armory, along the edge of the golf course in Lincoln Park ten or twelve blocks south of the zoo. I'm able to specify those locations because they were reported in the newspaper afterward. At the time, I had no more than my usual hazy childhood sense of where I was.

Bethie got out and opened the door to the back seat. "Come on," she told Danny and me. Even though I was still wailing and emotionally out of control for the second time that day, I was noticing things with uncanny precision. I saw the compassionate calm in my mother's eyes that told me I was not in trouble, only that she understood I needed comforting. I saw the glance she exchanged with Hugh, the wordless way she communicated that she needed to be alone with her children and his acknowledgment that he understood and would wait for us in the car for as long as she needed him to.

She took my hand, and Danny's hand, and led us onto the grassy verge on the side of the street, got down on one knee, and drew us to her and held us as tight as a mother could. I was still screaming, and my body was quaking, but I knew now that whatever had seized me would let me go, and that with my face pressed against my mother's shoulder there need be no hurry for it to happen.

We could not have stopped at a more random place, at the side of an obscure street that backed up to a golf course, whose green expanse was hidden by a narrow strip of dark woods. The day was fading, but the slowly setting sun flared on the unseen horizon, saturating everything around us with magical vividness and color.

"Shhh . . . shhh . . ." Bethie kept saying, and her voice seemed to me to have something to do with the way the light was gently failing, as if she were commanding the world to join her in soothing my distress.

In a moment I was better, but I was still wiping my tears against her shoulder as she stroked the top of my head. Danny had also unashamedly burrowed himself into her. I've lived a long and generally happy life, but I've never experienced since—and would never expect to experience—the same flooding contentment of that distant moment, when my mother had her arms locked around my brother and me and I could feel the fear being expelled from my body by the pressure of her embrace.

After a few more moments she let us go, and I asked,

remembering the sight of Frank and Emmett standing there in defeat as Hugh's car pulled away, "Are they going to be okay?"

"Of course, honey," she said. "Of course they're going to be okay. They won't be away long. They just made a mistake."

"Emmett shot a dog!" Danny said. His voice was loud and declarative. A moment earlier he had been a little boy clinging to his mother, just like me, but now he had recovered his status as a worldly big brother.

"I know he did," Bethie said. "But he didn't mean to. Are you boys ready to go home now? Are you feeling better, Grady?"

I nodded mutely, but none of us moved at first. Bethie, still crouched in front of us, a hand on my shoulder and the other on Danny's, looked away toward the car where Hugh was standing, leaning against the front bumper.

"Are you going to marry him?" Danny asked. The question came out of nowhere, startling me with its directness even more than it must have startled Bethie, because I had only a shadowy grasp of what marriage even meant. It brought home once more how much more powerful an understanding of the world my one-year-older brother had.

Bethie didn't answer at once. She sat back onto the weedy ground, gently holding our arms.

"Yes, I think so. What do you boys think of that idea?"

She saw us shrug and she smiled. "I think you both like him, don't you?"

I did like him, but I wasn't going to admit it. Danny slowly nodded his head, as if he had actually deliberated and made up his mind, rather than just watched passively as the adults in our lives made their decisions and swept us up in their consequences.

"Do you like him too, Grady?"

I didn't answer, because to do so would have felt like I was locking something of deadly importance into place, and there had already been too many momentous and confusing occurrences today.

"It's all right," she said. "You don't have to say anything. But you know something? Hugh likes you boys very much. He says you're—"

I wasn't listening anymore, not because I was uninterested, but because the sinking sun had spotlighted something twenty yards or so away, in the thin strip of scraggly forest. A patch of white verging on yellow, with smaller patches of black. It was something alive and moving, though the motion was slow and almost imperceptible, heaving and pulsing in place like the raincoat monster I thought I had seen that night in our hallway.

I had learned enough from that experience to know that my mind was capable of creating such hallucinatory images, so I assumed this was just another instance. In any case, this wasn't a monster, it wasn't scary, it was something sad and small and needful. I didn't say anything, I didn't call out. I just stared.

And Bethie saw me staring, and followed my gaze, and saw what I was looking at. She was still holding us, and I could feel a tremor run through her body, a bolt of pure fear like what I imagine she had experienced when she saw those uniformed Air Force personnel walking up to her door to tell her that her husband was dead. But in this case the spasm of fear lasted for only an instant. She didn't call out to anyone, she didn't grab Danny and me and run away in terror. She must have understood almost immediately that what she was seeing wasn't the nightmare beast she had imagined a few days earlier when she had run into the park, almost gasping with fright, to grab her children out of the sandbox and flee with them to shelter.

"Wait here," she said to us, almost in a whisper, and then she stood and walked cautiously forward, bending her head and pushing branches out of the way as she advanced a few yards into the narrow thicket-like growth. I saw her bend down very cautiously beside the thing that was lying there, the thing that I knew was the leopard. Everything was growing dark around her, but her nurse's uniform still glowed white, and the complex, vibrant color and patterning of the animal's fur was still bright.

She turned her head to look at Danny and me, and there were tears in her eyes. She said nothing, just silently gestured for us to join her. Up close, even to a child, the leopard looked small and helpless, nothing like the man-eating beast of Rudraprayag or the snarling predator the whole city had been on guard against, and not even recognizable as the restless animal we had witnessed trying to leap out of the leopard pit that day at the zoo. All its tensile strength was gone. It was thin and so weak I would not have been able to tell that it was alive if it hadn't been for the way its chest heaved with its panting and the thin white froth that kept pouring from its mouth.

"He's dying," Bethie whispered to us. I didn't know precisely what that meant, but as I looked down at the poisoned leopard I saw what it meant, and saw that there was nothing my mother could do but try to make it understand that it wasn't alone.

"It's all right," she said. She wasn't speaking to me, or to Danny, but to the leopard. She must have seen enough dying men during the war to know that the animal was past the point where it could harm her, that it was safe for her to touch it. She moved her hand forward, drew it back, moved it forward again until it was grazing the leopard's body. The creature's canine teeth were bared, and the one eye that was visible to me on the side of its head stared straight ahead at nothing. Danny reached out his hand as well. Bethie didn't stop him, and that gave me the courage to touch the leopard too, to run my fingers through the black rosettes on its fur and to feel the breath rapidly rising and falling through the hard bones in its rib cage.

"I'll be damned," I heard Hugh say. He was standing behind us now, at the edge of the woods.

Bethie turned to him and said, "Don't let anybody shoot it, Hugh."

"I won't," he said.

By now other cars had pulled up along the side of the road. Though we were in an out-of-the-way place, the roads were still full of vehicles driven by vigilant leopard hunters. The sight of a woman and children half-hidden in the trees, and a man nearby, all of them staring at something, must have attracted first one driver's attention, then another's. The result was that people came spilling out of their cars with shotguns and rifles, eager to see what might be going on. When they saw the leopard lying on the ground, Hugh didn't even need to say anything to them. They all seemed to understand it was pointless now to fire a shot at an animal that was already miserably dying.

The brakes squealed on one of the stopping cars and a man in a bow tie and a sport coat with sweat stains in the armpits jumped out and ran toward us, carrying an imposing-looking camera.

"Everybody stay right where you are!" he commanded as

he lurched to a stop and looked down through the camera's viewfinder. But in that moment the shot that he must have wanted, the shot of a pretty young nurse tending a dying leopard, ended up eluding him. Because as soon as she saw him, Bethie stepped out of his perfect composition, leaving Danny and me standing by ourselves with the terror of Oklahoma City stretched out at our feet. That's why the banner headline on the cover of *The Daily Oklahoman* the next day read "Leopard Found by OKC Boy Hunters."

23

Not much of what follows will be of any interest to the Oklahoma Historical Society, since what I've written so far is pretty much all the light that I'm capable of shedding on the Great Leopard Hunt. As anybody can find out from reading the newspapers for the week or so after the "capture," the leopard died after he had eaten horsemeat dosed with chloral hydrate that had been put out as bait near the zoo. But the dose had been far too strong. By the time the zoo's veterinarian arrived on the scene and tried to revive the animal by injecting him repeatedly with a stimulant, he was far too weak to respond and died only an hour after we encountered him.

It had been a dispiriting and anticlimactic ending to a great civic upheaval. The beast that so many citizens had feared, the trophy that all those hunters had been seeking, turned out in the end to have been an animal so disoriented and confused that he had killed nothing or no one, and had been found only a mile or so from the pit from which he had escaped and to which—in his hunger and fear—he had been trying to return, the only place of relative safety that he knew. The radio and television stations stopped referring to him as Leapy. Now that it was known that he hadn't harmed anybody and had died such a pitiful death, the insouciant nickname must have struck them as shameful.

The day our photo appeared in the newspaper, Frank and Emmett came home. Big Dan bailed them out and dropped Frank off at the Springlake parking lot to pick up his car. Bethie was making us lunch when we heard Emmett, and then a few minutes later Frank, walk up the stairway to their garage apartment. "The boys are home," she said, and left it at that. After that, I don't remember anybody ever speaking about why they had been gone or where they had been. And I don't remember anybody mentioning the other people who had gone to jail that day, the man we had heard referred to as Uncle Melvin and his sons and nephews. I'd like to think that someone from my family—Big Dan or even my uncles—had put in a call to the police to do what they could to get the charges withdrawn or reduced. Perhaps—maybe even probably—they had, though I doubt it would have helped, not in that time and that place.

Big Dan read us an article one morning at breakfast about what should be done with the leopard carcass. The leading idea was to make a fur coat out of the pelt and auction it off for charity, but I guess nothing ever came of that, because the leopard ended up being stuffed and put on display in the zoo.

Our grandfather took Danny and me to see it soon after it was presented to the public a few months later. Next to the concession stand at the zoo there was a kind of alcove where a viewing window opened onto a brand-new diorama display— jungle weeds set up against a painted backdrop of an African veldt with running antelope. (Never mind that Leapy had come from India.) In the middle of this panorama stood the leopard. He had been woefully diminished when we encountered him that night while he was dying, but now, stuffed and utterly motionless, he appeared even smaller. He had weighed two hundred pounds when he escaped from the zoo, but in the display he looked not much larger than a house cat. And he had been mounted rather artlessly, planted stiffly on his four legs without a suggestion of the startling agility we had witnessed that day at the zoo when he had tried to leap out of the pit.

There was a stuffed peacock lying on the ground in front of him—evidence of his killer's nature—but the leopard was configured in a way that suggested he took no notice of his prey. Instead, his head was turned toward the glass and, by accident or something more thought out, the taxidermist had imparted to him an expression of meek curiosity. He stared at the human onlookers—at us—as if he were trying to understand something.

"So that's what all the fuss was about." Big Dan chuckled as he stood behind us. He looked around for someone to talk to and proudly point out—as he had a hundred times already—that Danny and I were the ones who had found the leopard, but most of the zoo-goers were elsewhere, looking at live exhibits. I was glad we were spared this time. We were both already weary of fame, which brought nothing but annoying, repetitious questions and bursts of congratulation from the adults who crowded around us.

We saw the stuffed leopard sometime in the late fall of that year, after Bethie and Hugh were married in a quiet ceremony at our local church with only the family in attendance. After the wedding they had gone to Midland, where Hugh lived alone in a small apartment, to find a house for our new family of four. I knew that soon they would come back to Oklahoma City for Danny and me, and that we would move away. I had an imperfect awareness that these were counting-down days, and at the end of them a different world lay ahead, a world without daily proximity to the extended family I had always known.

There was much excited talk about that new life, about how big and exciting Texas was, about the new house where we would be living. But I knew that part of the excitement was manufactured, that it was part of a story that the adults were telling to reassure not just Danny and me but themselves. I could detect our grandparents watching us with a new intensity, as if they were trying to fix into their memories everything we did or said. I noticed how, out of the blue, Vivian was likely to erupt into what she called "tears of happiness." She was so thrilled, she said, that her sister had a new husband, and that her nephews had a new father, and that we were all moving to Texas.

"And don't you worry," she told us, "it's not like we won't see you anymore. We'll see you all the time! You'll only be a couple hundred miles away! Do you think I'd let you forget your dear old aunt Vivian?"

There was something different about Frank and Emmett too. Frank had found a new job, something I didn't understand having to do with the oil pipeline business, and that kept him out in the field at odd hours and often out of town. His absence helped to defuse the constant friction with Big Dan, though there were still nights when he came home very late and mornings when he hadn't come home at all, when Big Dan paced angrily in the driveway and stared at the place where his son's car was supposed to be.

It may have been my imagination that when Frank was at home, he kept a certain distance from Danny and me—but that was the disquieting, disappointing impression that I had. If he was consciously holding himself apart, was it because his nephews were an uncomfortable reminder of the perils to which we had been exposed by his negligence? Or—this is what I'd rather believe, and do believe—was he unconsciously inoculating himself against the pain of giving us up to another man, a man who he must have recognized, even as he couldn't help resenting him for it, would be our father?

Emmett was the opposite, as he was in most things when it came to his older brother. He would come down from his garage apartment almost every night, in those days before Bethie married Hugh, and help her with bedtime, and read us stories and kneel by the side of the bed with us as we said our prayers. It was almost as if he wanted to get as close to us as possible to intensify the pain of losing us when we went away.

He was the one who hugged us the tightest the day they all convened in the driveway to say goodbye before we drove away in Hugh's car. I'm not sure I fully processed that this was the end of something big. I don't remember taking a last lingering look around—at my grandparents' house and our apartment, or at the green park that seemed to spread into infinity beyond the gate with its recumbent metal dogs. The park still appears in my dreams, even now that I'm in my seventies when dreams of beckoning expanses have more to do with what comes after death than with the explosive discoveries of childhood. Emmett's grip was ferocious as he held us both. He didn't say much, just held on like that until he let us go.

Frank grabbed our heads and rubbed his knuckles across our scalps and mock-growled, trying to make us believe, and make himself believe, that this was an everyday goodbye. But his face was tight, and when he said "I'll see you boys around," his voice caught in his throat.

The whole family walked forward in the driveway as we pulled away, Babi and Vivian both vigorously weeping, Big Dan pacing stoically with his hands in his pockets, Frank and Emmett following all the way to the curb and then out into the middle of the street. I saw them the longest. It wasn't until we turned left onto Classen at the end of the block that they finally stopped waving.

I was cushioned by excitement, by what was to come. But the heavy, resigned way that my two uncles finally turned and began to walk back up the driveway took me by surprise and made me wonder—for one shivering moment—if this would be the last time I would ever see them.

It wasn't, though. Bethie had told us again and again as she prepared us for the move that we would always come back to see our family in Oklahoma City, and we always did, but I was beginning to see how the existence that had seemed to me permanently fixed was in fact set upon a slow floodtide of time. That current had carried us off to our new lives in Midland that day, and soon enough it would carry Vivian to a better and busier executive-assistant job in St. Louis, and from there to the Miami office of Cunard Line and a long career cruising around the world and never bothering to get married. ("Just never had a spare moment," she happily told us.) When Frank married Beverly, a year after we left, it was a justice-of-the-peace wedding that probably had something to do with him declaring to his rigorously Catholic parents that he would be doing things his own way from now on. He and Beverly moved to Anadarko to be closer to his company's headquarters. They never had children, but I had the impression that the two of them were enough for each other and happy together, living close enough to the family in Oklahoma City that they could drop in for Sunday dinner and drive back that same afternoon. There may have been other tense moments from time to time between Frank and Big Dan, but I never witnessed them. As Frank grew more successful and indispensable at the pipeline company, he stopped drinking so much. And there were times, in the years before Big Dan's death, when I saw the two of them talking easily and affectionately to each other—father to son—on the front porch after Sunday dinner. Our trips back to Oklahoma City were always crowded with family activities, and we never had a chance to visit Frank and Beverly in Anadarko. The only time I saw their house was at the funeral reception after Frank was killed in a pipeline explosion at the age of forty-eight. It hadn't been a Catholic service, but the funeral home had found a rosary in his pocket.

It was different with Emmett. We saw him all the time when we returned to Oklahoma City—or "home," as Bethie never stopped calling it. He married Rose rather late in life, after he had already become a successful oil-and-gas attorney, but not so late to get in the way of them having four children together. Toward the end of his life, when he was in his eighties and suffering from Alzheimer's, unexpected noises could still send him into a spiral of fearful confusion, and to calm him his children would always lead him to the garage he had converted many years before into his art studio. He had a very modest, regional-art-fair sort of reputation, and once there was even an article about him—"Meet the Attorney Who Is Our Local

Van Gogh"—in the newspaper. But as his illness progressed, blank canvases started to make him nervous. That's when one of my cousins had the idea of buying him one of those paint-by-number kits they sell in hobby shops. He followed the instructions and painstakingly filled in the minute numbered spaces with the appropriate colors, but there was still something so unusual about the finished products—an eerie sense of energy and commitment, combined with the fact that he always left one of the tiny numbered spaces unpainted—that several of his painter friends even wanted to buy them. I was in the crowded room with him a few years ago when he died, and so was Danny, who had cut short a long-planned Tanzanian photo safari with his two sons and rushed back to Oklahoma City to say goodbye. Bethie was there too, ninety-one years old, holding her little brother's hand.

When his children were clearing out his studio, they found a manila folder labeled "Danny and Grady" in an old man's shaking handwriting. Inside were two completed paint-by-number canvases of a leopard in the jungle.

"We're coming up to the Red River," I remember Hugh telling us the day we left Oklahoma City. By that time, we had been driving south for two or three hours. To try to keep us from constantly whining in boredom from the back seat, Bethie had instructed us to play Zip, a car game her parents had played with her when she was a young girl in Kansas. You kept your eyes peeled on the roadside and said "Zip" whenever you saw a white horse. It's an unworkable game these days, since there are very few white horses anymore in an enclosing landscape of suburbs and strip malls. But it worked well enough that day to keep us calm and occupied for about twenty minutes, until Danny and I got into a fight over who had seen the white horse first.

We were still bouncing around, restless with confinement and excitement, when we came to the Red River. It was disappointing. I had built up in my mind what it would be like to leave Oklahoma, had imagined some sort of monumental border-crossing experience that would throw me into a different world. Instead, there was a bridge over a shallow, spread-out, muddy-pink expanse of water. And ahead was nothing special, either—just a Welcome sign shaped like the state of Texas, and then more of the same wintry plains. Nothing to see, not even a white horse so that I could call out "Zip." Nothing more to do to occupy myself, except to remember what we had left behind and to wonder what lay ahead.

Acknowledgments

When I published my first novel, in 1980, it wasn't customary to include an acknowledgments page at the end of the book. Those were the days when writers were still conditioned to regard their work as an act of sheer creative autonomy. It's true enough that it's our job alone, or should be, to write the actual sentences, but before we set down a word we're often already indebted to friends, family members, publishing professionals, and helpful strangers who have made it possible for us to reach the starting place. And when we finally have written something we think is good enough for others to read, when it's time to turn those manuscript pages into a book, there is a hidden host of people waiting to take it off our hands and make it real.

While I'm writing a book I keep a running list of people who have helped me along the way, and that list usually begins with my longtime agent and friend, Esther Newberg, of ICM. Esther is the first link in the chain of custody by which my pages end up in the superb care of my longtime editor and friend, Ann Close. I'd also like to thank Esther's ICM colleague Estie Berkowitz and, at Knopf, Ann's colleague—and now associate editor—Todd Portnowitz.

I wrote this book, but Knopf made it, and it has been my good fortune for over forty years to be backed by the best publisher that ever existed. It's not just a courtesy, but a moral necessity, to thank everyone on the team that I've come into even glancing contact with on the production of *The Leopard Is Loose*: Reagan Arthur, of course, and Nicholas Latimer, Paul Bogaards, my publicist Gabrielle Brooks, media specialist Sara Eagle, and Demetri Papadimitropoulos. Kevin Bourke saw the book through the production process and Soonyoung Kwon designed its interior. I'm also very grateful to Jenny Carrow for her inviting cover design and Patrick Dillon for his thoughtful copy editing and—once or twice—crucial fact-checking.

My books ideas often emerge out of spitballing sessions with old friends that include Lawrence Wright, William Broyles, Gregory Curtis, H. W. Brands, and Jim Magnuson. In this case, both Larry and Bill read the manuscript beforehand and made suggestions that helped me see it anew. And as always, I leaned on Elizabeth Crook for her unerring guidance and lasting friendship.

For the factual background of this novel, I'm indebted to insights from Neal Spelce, Lee Yeakel, Bill Crook, Alan Huffines, Daniel Okrent, Patrick Crocker, Vladislav Zidek, and Victor Emanuel. A chance encounter with Katie Maratta and her husband S. C. Gwynne as we were walking around Lady Bird Lake in Austin led to Katie's suggestion for the book's title.

My brother Jim Harrigan read the manuscript as well and made suggestions which—as a dutiful younger brother—I was happy to accept. I also enlisted my cousins Bob Berney and Lou Berney for their thoughts about the story and their memories of Oklahoma City.

The Oklahoma Historical Society was an important source not just for information about the leopard escape but about race relations in the 1950s, and about civil rights leaders like Clara Luper and Jimmy Stewart. Alex Kershaw's *The Liberator* was the main source when it came to conjuring up a World War II background for one of my characters.

Immensely helpful to me in supplementing my own memories

of Oklahoma City places, restaurants, architecture, etc., were the remarkable local history books from Arcadia Publishing.

Sue Ellen Harrigan, to whom I've been married for forty-six years, hasn't read this book yet. We have an agreement that, since I crave her approval too much, and since the slightest unintended gesture or inflection that could be interpreted as negative would crush me, it's better that she read my books after they're published. As ever, I nervously await her verdict.

Since this book is told through the point of view of a five-year-old boy, I was able to draw upon not only my memories of childhood, but of parenthood, when I observed with a kind of blessed intensity our three daughters—Marjorie, Dorothy, and Charlotte—as they were growing up. Now that Sue Ellen and I have six grandchildren, we are witnessing the magic and fears of childhood once again at close range. They don't know it, but those grandchildren—Mason, Travis, Maisie, Romy, Sonny, and Gladys—helped me write this book.

A NOTE ABOUT THE AUTHOR

Stephen Harrigan's previous novels include the *New York Times* best-selling *The Gates of the Alamo, Remember Ben Clayton* (which, among other awards, won the James Fenimore Cooper Prize from the Society of American Historians for best historical novel), and *A Friend of Mr. Lincoln*. He has also written a number of books of nonfiction, including the recent *Big Wonderful Thing: A History of Texas* and a career-spanning collection of essays, *The Eye of the Mammoth*. He is a writer-at-large for *Texas Monthly* as well as a screenwriter who has written many movies for television.

A NOTE ON THE TYPE

This book was set in Scala, a typeface designed by the Dutch designer Martin Majoor (b. 1960) in 1988 and released by the FontFont foundry in 1990. While designed as a fully modern family of fonts containing both a serif and a sans serif alphabet, Scala retains many refinements normally associated with traditional fonts.

Composed by North Market Street Graphics,
Lancaster, Pennsylvania

Printed and bound by Berryville Graphics,
Berryville, Virginia

Designed by Soonyoung Kwon